Justin grazed her cheek with his knuckles.

Longing shimmered through her, a deep yearning for more than that gentle touch. For now, though—perhaps forever—more was forbidden.

"Thank you," Patsy said breathlessly. "I enjoyed the walk and the ice cream."

In fact, she had enjoyed the whole evening entirely too much. It had made her want things that she couldn't have.

Tonight had proved beyond any doubt that being around Justin Adams was dangerous. One day soon he wouldn't settle for the quick brush of his fingers, as he was doing now.

Worse, one day soon, she wouldn't, either.

Dear Reader,

It's the most festive time of the year! And Special Edition is celebrating with six sparkling romances for you to treasure all season long.

Those MORGAN'S MERCENARIES are back by popular demand with bestselling author Lindsay McKenna's brand-new series, MORGAN'S MERCENARIES: THE HUNTERS. Book one, *Heart of the Hunter,* features the first of four fearless brothers who are on a collision course with love—and danger. And in January, the drama and adventure continues with Lindsay's provocative Silhouette Single Title release, *Morgan's Mercenaries: Heart of the Jaguar.*

Popular author Penny Richards brings you a poignant THAT'S MY BABY! story for December. In *Their Child,* a ranching heiress and a rugged rancher are married for the sake of *their* little girl, but their platonic arrangement finally blossoms into a passionate love. Also this month, the riveting PRESCRIPTION: MARRIAGE medical miniseries continues with an unlikely romance between a mousy nurse and the man of her secret dreams in *Dr. Devastating* by Christine Rimmer. And don't miss Sherryl Woods's 40th Silhouette novel, *Natural Born Lawman,* a tale about two willful opposites attracting—the latest in her AND BABY MAKES THREE: THE NEXT GENERATION miniseries.

Just in time for the holidays, award-winning author Marie Ferrarella delivers a *Wife in the Mail*—a heartwarming story about a gruff widower who falls for his brother's jilted mail-order bride. And long-buried family secrets are finally revealed in *The Secret Daughter* by Jackie Merritt, the last book in THE BENNING LEGACY crossline miniseries.

I hope you enjoy all our romance novels this month. All of us at Silhouette Books wish you a wonderful holiday season!

Sincerely,
Karen Taylor Richman
Senior Editor

Please address questions and book requests to:
Silhouette Reader Service
U.S.: 3010 Walden Ave., P.O. Box 1325, Buffalo, NY 14269
Canadian: P.O. Box 609, Fort Erie, Ont. L2A 5X3

SHERRYL WOODS
NATURAL BORN LAWMAN

Published by Silhouette Books
America's Publisher of Contemporary Romance

SILHOUETTE BOOKS

ISBN 0-373-24216-6

NATURAL BORN LAWMAN

Copyright © 1998 by Sherryl Woods

Printed in U.S.A.

Books by Sherryl Woods

SHERRYL WOODS

can't be far from the sea without getting downright claustrophobic. She's lived by the ocean on both coasts and now divides her time between Key Biscayne, Florida, and her childhood summer home in Colonial Beach, Virginia. She spends much of her time writing books about falling in love and living happily ever after. *Natural Born Lawman* is her fortieth novel for Silhouette! She loves to hear from readers and can be reached at P.O. Box 490326, Key Biscayne, FL 33149.

ADAMS FAMILY TREE

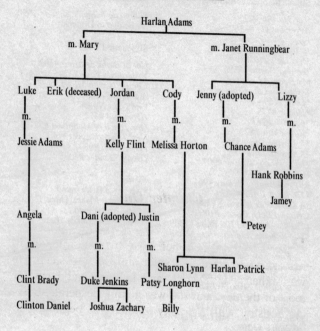

Chapter One

Patsy Longhorn held her fussy two-year-old son in her arms and tried to soothe him back to sleep. He was exhausted, feverish and hungry, had been for most of the day, and she was getting desperate. Driving nonstop with a cranky toddler was beginning to take its toll.

She hadn't intended to take another break yet. She'd wanted to put as much distance between herself and Oklahoma as she possibly could today, but she hadn't been able to ignore Billy's whimpers a second longer. She'd pulled into a rest stop and taken him out of his car seat, praying that holding him and rocking him a bit would accomplish what her pitiful repertoire of lullabies hadn't.

So far it wasn't working. Worse, he felt warmer, as if his fever had gone up a little more.

"Come on, sweetie, go to sleep. You'll feel better after you've had a little rest."

At least she prayed that was all it would take. She didn't have money left for medicine and a doctor at this point. Even juice was stretching her tight budget. She'd been giving him sips of cool water and praying that would do the trick.

Billy shifted restlessly, still whimpering, his dark, dark eyes staring back at her, accusing her. Guilt, never far away, washed over her again.

Had she made a mistake leaving Will? Was she crazy to have walked out on her marriage? Walked out with only clothes for the baby and herself and a few hundred dollars from the checking account she had opened several months earlier and had kept secret from her husband?

Though she'd had every right, she hadn't touched a dime in their joint account for fear Will would accuse her of theft. With her name on the account the wild charge wouldn't stick, of course, but she hadn't wanted to give the police any excuses at all to chase after her. It was terrifying enough that Will was likely to go ballistic.

That, she reminded herself staunchly, was exactly the reason she had left. She'd had no choice. Will's temper was out of control. He never talked anymore. He shouted, he threw things. A vase had whizzed past her head, just a few nights ago, only inches from making contact. The violence in his eyes had terrified her. He hadn't hit her or their son yet, but she'd heard enough about abuse to know that it was coming. She wasn't going to stick around and wait for it, not when each scene was already escalating to a more dangerous level.

Nor was she going to waste time trying to convince Will to seek counseling. His pride and his very visible career would never allow him to admit he needed help. For once in her life, she was doing the smart thing. She was going to cut her losses before tragedy struck.

She hadn't been so smart when she'd impetuously moved to Oklahoma City and almost immediately begun an affair with Will Longhorn. Barely nineteen, she'd been so anxious to get away from home and her overly protective parents, to be on her own. The irony was that she'd spent hardly a minute truly on her own before becoming entangled with Will.

He had been her first boss, a twenty-six-year-old attorney in the town's top law firm with a dazzling career ahead of him. Everyone had said so. He was a Native American with the whole world spread out before him. There'd even been talk of a run for political office, first in Oklahoma, then for Congress. Will Longhorn had charisma. He was smart. He had unblemished integrity, as well, a rarity in politics.

And before too terribly long, he had a beautiful, blond-haired, all-American wife at his side and a baby on the way. The image had been set, the campaign posters all but printed.

At first Patsy had been thrilled to be a part of it all. She'd been caught up in every girl's dream. She had been so proud of her handsome husband, so in love with him.

But all too soon, behind the public displays of affection, behind the jovial smiles for the camera, there had been the private dissension. Even as he showcased his trophy wife and beautiful baby boy, privately Will seemed to resent both Patsy and their son. And because she had given up her job to be a stay-at-home wife and mom, she was totally dependent on Will for everything. It was what he'd wanted, but he'd thrown that back in her face a time or two, as well.

In general the abuse was subtle and mostly verbal, but it was signal enough to her that it was time to go. She might have married in haste, but she had no intention of paying for it for the rest of her life. And no one was going to harm her son. No one.

Protecting Billy became her first priority. Already in his young life, he had heard too much fighting, witnessed too many vicious arguments. If she and Will couldn't live together peacefully, if not lovingly, then it was time to go.

She had fled first to her parents, but Will had followed and the scene he'd caused had terrified all of them. He'd bashed the headlights on her car, dented the hood with a blow of his fists. He'd threatened her, accused her of trying to ruin his career, their future. He'd threatened her parents, blamed them for harboring his wife when she belonged at home with him. Her parents were just old-fashioned enough to agree that a wife's place was at her husband's side, no matter the circumstances. She had seen the unspoken agreement in their eyes, but still she had balked at leaving.

And then Will had sealed her fate. He had calmly vowed to take Billy away from her if she didn't agree to come home with him.

"You won't even get weekend visitations by the time I'm through. I can do it," he'd said with cool cruelty in his eyes. "You know I can."

She hadn't doubted it for an instant. She had gone with him simply to keep her baby and to get Will away from her frightened family.

Satisfied that he'd gotten his way, Will had promptly gone back on the campaign trail in the mayoral race that was to be the stepping-stone to his entire political future. And the low-key pattern of denigration had begun again—the sarcastic barbs, the ruthless demands, the never-ending criticism. She had taken it for six more humiliating months while she secretly made her plans. And all the while she watched Will, waiting for an explosion of temper that always came.

This time when she'd left, she had known that wherever she went, she was on her own. A local shelter had provided a safe harbor for a day or two. Then she had turned the car toward Texas, hoping that simply crossing the line into another state might offer her some protection. Too many cops, too many judges, too many politicians in Oklahoma owed favors to Will or to the partners in his law firm. Even though she'd worked there, if it came to a choice between her and Will, she had no doubt which of them would receive the partners' backing.

The memory of that violent explosion in front of her parents' home in full view of the neighbors had kept her on the run for a week now, trying to decide where it would be safe to settle down and begin an anonymous life. While in Oklahoma, she hadn't dared to stay even in a cheap motel for more than a good night's sleep.

As of today, her options were running out. Her pitiful savings were pretty much wiped out and she didn't dare phone her parents for help. For all she knew Will would have bugged their phone. It wasn't beyond him to use the law to his own advantage, especially when her second disappearance at the height of his first campaign for office was no doubt causing him a great deal of public embarrassment.

This time she was truly on her own, for the first time in her life, and the decisions she made were critical not only to her own future, but to the baby's. This was the ultimate test any woman could face. How she handled it would prove what she was made of. So far, she feared, she was falling pitifully short, but she was determined to pull it together. She might be almost out of money and be running low on ideas, but the one thing Patsy Gresham Longhorn had was gumption.

Billy whimpered, reminding her that she was going to have to come to a decision in a hurry. He needed food and, quite possibly, medical attention, though she was pretty sure the fever was little more than a summer cold.

With the two-year-old still cuddled in her arms, she

tried awkwardly to unfold the road map she'd picked up at an earlier highway rest stop. Dallas was close, but was a big city the best choice? Wouldn't the police there be on the lookout for her, if Will had spread the word that she was missing?

A small town with more casual, less experienced law enforcement seemed a safer bet. If her logic was faulty, so be it. She felt more at ease with the thought of trying to make a home for herself and Billy someplace quiet and peaceful, someplace where they'd never heard of Will Longhorn. Her gut instincts had gotten her this far. She might as well trust them a little longer.

Staring at the choices on the map, all of them unfamiliar, she finally zeroed in on a tiny speck in the southwestern part of the state: Los Piños. It was only a couple of hundred miles away. The name suggested forests of pine trees, which appealed to her. She craved the serenity such a setting suggested. It reminded her of the town where she'd grown up, the town she'd been in too much of a hurry to leave. Funny, what a difference a few agonizing years could make. She would have given almost anything to be able to go back there now. Since she couldn't, it would have to be Los Piños.

The decision made, she got back on the highway, then took the next exit and stopped at a minimart to buy milk and some cereal for the baby and a ready-made sandwich and soft drink for her. After filling the car with gas, she had ten dollars left, that and whatever change might be buried in the bottom of her purse and in Billy's diaper bag.

Despite the dire circumstances, Patsy felt almost upbeat as she drove into Los Piños a few hours later. She gazed around at the small downtown area with its quaint shops and family-owned restaurants. Though the buildings were old, everything was freshly painted and brightly lit. There was no mistaking that this was a town that took pride in itself. For a second she allowed herself to envision being a part of it, to imagine belonging. For a moment anyway, despair vanished. A feeling of contentment, mixed with a rare smidgen of hope, stole over her.

"We're here, Billy," she whispered to the now-sleeping boy. "We're home." Whatever it took, she would find a way to make that true.

She reached into the back seat and touched his cheek to seal the vow, then drew back in shock. He was burning up with fever. Hope gave way to panic and desperation.

"It'll be okay, baby," she promised. Whatever she had to do, it would be okay.

"Dadgumit, Justin, if you'd been the law around here when we were kids, I'd have spent my entire teens in jail," Harlan Patrick Adams grumbled, standing on a corner in downtown Los Piños just before dinnertime.

Justin grinned at his cousin. "Probably should have," he said.

"You were no better than me," Harlan Patrick reminded him. "If I belonged in a cell, you surely belonged right there next to me. What happened to you? When did you turn into a saint?"

"Hardly that," Justin said. "It's just that there's right and wrong. Somebody's got to see to it that folks remember the difference."

"Yeah, but that kid you just threatened with jail time threw a gum wrapper on the street. He didn't rob the savings and loan."

"Stop the little crime and you'll have less trouble with the big stuff," Justin retorted. "That's what that mayor up in New York says and it's worked."

"It makes my blood run cold hearing you talk like that," Harlan Patrick taunted. "Guess that means you won't be playing poker with the rest of us out at White Pines later tonight, seeing as how gambling's illegal. Or were you thinking of coming along and arresting Grandpa Harlan when he rakes in his first pot?"

Justin scowled at him. "Very amusing. I'll be there and I intend to take every dime you lay on the table, cowboy."

Harlan Patrick didn't appear unduly worried. "Just as long as you leave that gun locked up at home," he said. "It makes me very nervous to know that you're carrying a weapon. You never could shoot worth a damn."

Justin grinned and fingered his holster. "I'm better now. Want to see?"

Harlan Patrick shuddered. "I think I'll pass,

thanks.'' He gave Justin a mock salute. ''Later, cousin.''

''Yeah, later.''

After all their years of troublemaking, Justin got a kick out of watching Harlan Patrick squirm at the sight of his uniform. No one in the family, least of all his own father, quite understood what had motivated him to become a sheriff's deputy. Jordan Adams had saved a spot in his oil company for Justin and he was mad as hell that his son had turned it down. Justin figured his brother-in-law would settle into the position just fine and sooner or later everyone would get over his defection.

Ironically, it was the family's very own values that had taken root in Justin's heart and made him long to keep the whole community of Los Piños as safe and secure as his family was on their various ranches. In the cutthroat oil business, his father had a straight-arrow reputation for honesty and never cutting corners. Grandpa Harlan's instinctive decency and tough-love brand of justice were as ingrained in Justin as breathing. Even as a kid, when he and Harlan Patrick had played cops and robbers, he'd always, *always* wanted to be the good guy. To him, becoming a cop was less a surprise than a destiny.

He stood on the sidewalk in the middle of town after his cousin had gone and surveyed his domain. Not a bit of trouble in sight. Not even a gum wrapper on the sidewalk, he observed, smiling at the memory of that kid's expression as he'd snatched up the offending piece of paper and thrown it into the litter basket on the corner. His actions had been accompanied by a stern lecture meant to put the fear of God into the boy.

Yep, Justin thought, all was right in his world. Maybe he could actually get fifteen minutes to himself to grab a burger at Dolan's before it closed for the night. He radioed Becky at the station.

"I'll be at Dolan's, if you need me. Want me to bring you anything back?"

"A hamburger, double fries and a milk shake," the very pregnant receptionist said with heartfelt longing.

Coached on her dietary restraints by her worried husband, Justin asked, "How about a tuna on rye and a diet soda?"

Becky sighed. "It'll do."

"Ten-four."

As he walked down the block, he spotted the dusty, expensive car with the out-of-state tags. Los Piños didn't get a lot of tourists. He glanced around for some sign of strangers, but everyone out in the heat of the day was familiar. He shrugged and walked on after making a mental note of the tag number.

Inside the drugstore, he glanced at the counter, expecting to see Harlan Patrick's sister, Sharon Lynn. His cousin had taken over a job once held by her mother and now was thinking of buying out Doc Dolan so he could finally retire. If she actually went through with it, she would hire a new pharmacist and continue running the rest of the store as she had been for the past couple of years anyway.

"Hey, Sharon Lynn, you in here?" he called out,

even as he dragged a notebook from his pocket and wrote down the Oklahoma tag number.

"Back here, Justin," she replied from the back of the drugstore. "I'll be with you in a sec."

He'd barely settled on a stool at the counter, when he heard what sounded like a whispered argument. His cop's instincts, already alerted by the out-of-state car, kicked in. Drawing his gun, he moved silently down the aisle in the direction of the voices.

At the end of the row of shelves, he spotted Sharon Lynn and another woman, her blond hair scooped up into a careless ponytail, damp tendrils curling and clinging to her neck. The desperate expression on the stranger's face spelled trouble.

She was talking so fast he couldn't make heads or tails of what she was saying, but he didn't waste time trying to figure it out. While she was distracted, he moved in beside her and laid a restraining hand on her shoulder. Though she was dressed in expensive, tasteful clothes, she was so thin he could feel her bones. At his touch, she jolted as if she'd been shot, her panicked eyes clashing with his. It all added up to the kind of vulnerability that could make a man lose sight of the job he was being paid to do.

Keeping her firmly in his grip, he glanced at Sharon Lynn. "Everything okay?"

The stranger's eyes pleaded with his cousin. Sharon Lynn touched her hand gently.

"It's okay. Justin's my cousin. He's not going to hurt you."

"That all depends," Justin said, contradicting her. "What happened?"

"I needed some children's Tylenol," the woman said in a voice barely above a whisper. "My son's sick."

Sharon Lynn sighed. "I caught her trying to slip them into her purse," she admitted with obvious reluctance.

Justin tried not to react to the tears that were welling up in the woman's eyes, turning them into huge pools of green light, like sunshine reflected in a pond surrounded by tall pines. She was little more than twenty, it seemed to him, and fragile as a bird. He had a feeling if she was shoplifting Tylenol, then she hadn't had much to spend on food lately, either. Just because her clothes were pricey didn't mean she wasn't truly down on her luck. At the thought of the sick child, his rock-solid value system shifted ever so slightly. He felt justice clashing with compassion. Because he had a sudden, uncharacteristic instinct to bend some rules, his next words came out more harshly than he'd intended.

"Where's the boy?" he demanded gruffly.

"In the car."

He fought to hold his temper in check. "You left the baby in the car by himself? As hot as it is out there today?" And why, he wondered, hadn't he spotted the kid if he'd been securely strapped into a car seat as he should have been? He hadn't even checked inside the car. Obviously he was slipping.

"He's okay. I left the windows open a little. He's

sound asleep. Besides, I knew I'd only be gone a minute.'' She stared at him defiantly. ''You don't have to tell me all the terrible things that could happen. Believe me, I know. I weighed every one of them and decided he'd be safer there than with me. I didn't want him to cry and draw attention to me.'' Her shoulders sagged. ''It didn't matter. I really am no good at this.''

''Get him,'' Justin said tightly. ''Now.''

The instant he released her, the woman scooted past him and out the door.

''She'll run,'' Sharon Lynn said, staring at him in astonishment.

''No, she won't,'' Justin said.

''How can you be so sure?''

He held up the package. ''Not without medicine.'' He handed his cousin a ten-dollar bill. ''Pay for them out of this, okay?''

Sharon Lynn gaped. ''Are you all right?''

''Just take the damned money.''

She grinned. ''Yes, sir.''

''And then fix a couple of milk shakes. I'll grab some juice for the baby.''

''Uh-oh,'' Sharon Lynn said. ''What did it, Justin? Those big green eyes or the tears?''

''Go to hell.''

''You ought to be nicer to me,'' she taunted. ''I can tell this story far and wide by morning. Grandpa Harlan will know every touching detail by the time you get there tonight for the poker game. Your life won't be worth living by the time they finish teasing you about letting a nasty, evil shoplifter off the hook just because she was beautiful.''

''You know, Sharon Lynn, there are things about you that old Kyle Mason doesn't know about,'' he said grimly, referring to her fiancé. ''That man's been dangling on the hook for the past fifty million years, it seems like, waiting for you to marry him. Could be I know just the way to cut him loose before the latest wedding date next month.''

''You wouldn't dare,'' she breathed.

He could see her calculating the risks and twisted the knife a little more. ''Wouldn't dare tell him that you were the party girl of your senior class at ole Los Piños High? Wouldn't dare mention that you landed in jail on your senior trip?'' he taunted. ''Try me.''

''Kyle knows all that,'' she said airily. ''He loves me anyway. Besides, you know perfectly well what kind of party girl I was, all talk.''

''So you say.''

Her gaze shifted toward the front window. ''If you ask me you'd do a whole lot better to be worrying about why your suspect appears to be about to pull out of the space in front and hightail it out of town.'' She shot him a smug look. ''Just the way I predicted she would.''

Justin looked up in time to see a car shoot backward into traffic amid a squeal of tires. As he'd expected, it was the fancy car with the out-of-state tags.

''Well, hell,'' he muttered, and took off running, the carton of juice he'd just grabbed still clutched in his hand.

"If you catch her, tell her I'm not pressing charges," Sharon Lynn shouted after him, laughing.

"If I catch her, I'm throwing her in jail," he vowed. "You give me a reason, even an itsy-bitsy reason, and you'll be in the cell right next to her."

Chapter Two

Patsy wasn't sure why she'd run. Obviously she hadn't wanted to be hauled off to jail, something that the sheriff's deputy had seemed perfectly capable of doing. But it was more than that. Fleeing had been instinctive, which told her quite a lot about the damage even a few days on the run had done to her normally assertive personality.

Seeing the judgment in the deputy's eyes, the disdain, ordinarily would have infuriated her enough to make her stand her ground. She was capable of holding her own in an argument, or at least she had been until living with Will had taught her that silence was often the only way to escape from escalating tensions.

One look at the deputy had told her that arguments would be wasted on him, too. There was an unyielding air about him, the kind of steadfast determination that would be great if he were on your side, not so terrific if he weren't.

She had been startled when he'd released her and sent her after Billy. Grateful for the unexpected opportunity to escape, she had seized it, not pausing to consider just how incensed the deputy might be by her actions.

Maybe the woman in the store could calm him down and keep him from chasing after her, she thought hopefully. Patsy had seen the compassion in the woman's eyes, had known that she was only a hairsbreadth from getting both the medicine and her freedom when the man had turned up. Though she hated taking advantage of anyone's kindness, she had been relieved that Billy would have the medicine he needed. That was all that really mattered.

Now, not only did she not have anything to bring her son's fever down, but she was a criminal, with an attempted shoplifting charge pending if that deputy decided to pursue matters.

For all she knew there were kidnapping charges on file back in Oklahoma, too. Will was perfectly capable of doing something so despicable just to make a point to her, to prove that he was the one with all the power. What would turn up if the deputy happened to catch her tag number and run it through his computer? There was no telling.

She couldn't take any chances that he might find something damaging. She would just have to drive faster and more cleverly than she ever had before.

Suiting her actions to her thoughts, she skidded onto the highway and headed north, back toward Dallas, after all. She would exit a few miles ahead, then take back roads to elude any pursuit.

Though her plight was increasingly desperate, she reminded herself that she still had a bank card with her. Though there was a risk that Will would use any transactions with it to track her, she would use it to get cash if there were no options left to her. She could get enough money to last a few more days, until she could find another town, maybe get a job and find a safe place for herself and Billy. It might even be smarter to abandon the car and fly to another state. If she used cash for the tickets, it would make the job of tracking her more difficult. It was a huge country and Will's reach surely couldn't extend to every corner of it.

When the car sputtered then chugged to a stop barely ten miles outside of Los Piños, she realized that in her rush to get away from the deputy, she'd made a terrible miscalculation. The blasted car was out of gas. It hardly mattered that she had the credit card or a few dollars left in her purse. She hadn't passed a gas station heading out of town. It was impossible to know how far ahead the next one might be.

That was the only reason, she assured herself, that Justin whoever-he-was-lawman caught up with her. He found her on the side of the road, cursing a blue streak about the gas-guzzling car Will had insisted she have, and rocking the fussy toddler in her arms. His reflective sunglasses prevented her from getting a good look at his eyes, but his I-told-you-so smile said it all. He'd never doubted for a moment that he'd catch up with her and haul her into custody.

"Get in," he ordered, gesturing toward the patrol car.

"You're arresting me?" she asked, as if it were the most ridiculous notion she'd ever heard. Will had been a master of haughty indignation and she had learned by example.

Their gazes clashed, hers defiant, his unreadable.

"No," he said finally with a heavy sigh. "I'm taking you back into town. Unless you'd prefer to stand around here and wait for someone else to come along and offer you a lift. I'll tell you right now, though, that it's a very long way to the next town and hardly anybody uses this particular stretch of road."

Patsy had guessed as much. Not a single car had passed by while she'd been standing beside the car, cursing her lousy luck.

"Sooner or later..." she began, thinking anything would be better than going someplace with this hard, no-nonsense man.

"Are you willing to take that chance? If your son's sick, this heat won't help."

Her resolve wavered. "But the car..."

"Isn't going anywhere," he said. "I'll have someone bring out some gas and drive it back into town."

"I could wait," she suggested hopefully.

"I don't think so."

"Then you are arresting me."

"Dammit, no. Like I said, I am just trying to get you and the baby out of this blazing heat."

"Oh."

He opened the door to the front seat, which reassured her slightly. If he were arresting her, surely she'd be locked securely in the back. He tossed the bottle of Tylenol over to her, then indicated the carton of juice on the seat. "I brought those along for your boy."

So he did have a heart, after all. Patsy swallowed hard against the tears that threatened. It was enough lure to get her inside. "Thank you."

He closed the door, then went around to the driver's side. When he was behind the wheel, he said, "There's a milk shake in the holder there. You look as if you could use it."

Patsy shook her head, unwilling to be too indebted to this man who so clearly—and justifiably—disapproved of her. "No, thanks."

He rolled his eyes at her deliberate contrariness. "Suit yourself."

The drive into town was made in uncomfortable silence. She waited for another explosion of temper or a stern lecture, but instead he glanced over at Billy, who was belted into the seat with her, no doubt a bending of the rules he was so fond of enforcing. He hadn't argued with her, though, or insisted she get his car seat and put him in the back.

"Is he okay? Are you sure you don't want to get him to a doctor?" he asked. "There's a hospital in

Garden City. I could run you over to the emergency room there."

"No," she said in a rush. When he shot a sharp-eyed look at her, she explained, "He'll be fine, once his fever goes down. He's just tired and fussy. I think he's getting a bit of a cold."

"Okay, if you're sure."

"I am."

The same uneasy silence fell again. Billy squirmed in her lap. "Mama?"

"Yes, baby."

Billy stared back at her with fever-bright eyes, then looked over at the man behind the wheel. "Who's that?"

"He's a policeman. He's helping us."

"Nice 'liceman," Billy murmured approvingly and fell back asleep.

Patsy glanced up just in time to catch a fleeting smile at the corners of Justin's mouth.

"At least the boy knows when someone's on his side," he commented.

She regarded him doubtfully. "Are you on my side, Deputy …?"

"Adams," he supplied. "Justin Adams. And as long as you don't break any laws, yes." He gave her a sharp look. "So far you haven't, at least not technically."

"Just because I got caught."

"Be grateful that my cousin has a forgiving nature. She won't press charges."

"Is that the only reason you're letting me off so easy?"

"Yes," he said curtly.

Patsy studied him intently, then shook her head. Her opinion of the man had undergone several drastic shifts since he'd turned up with the juice and medicine. "I don't think so. I think that under that by-the-book exterior beats the heart of a genuinely nice guy."

She was almost convinced he was a man she could trust. Even after he'd caught her stealing, even after she'd fled, he had thought first of her sick child. She could see, though, that the compliment made him uncomfortable. Maybe the leniency didn't fit his own image of himself.

"What's wrong, Deputy? Afraid if word gets out, it'll ruin your reputation?" she asked, daring to tease him, hoping to catch another glimpse of that potentially devastating smile again.

"Something like that," he conceded, unsmiling.

Patsy felt an odd little shock of disappointment, then cursed herself. Was she so desperate for a friend that she was willing to trust this stranger who had the power to give her whereabouts away to her husband? He was clearly a man with a strong sense of right and wrong, a commitment to duty. He would be the worst possible choice for a friend. When it came to a choice between obligation and friendship, there would be no contest. He would choose obligation every time.

She withdrew into silence once again.

"Where are you two heading?" he asked eventually.

The question seemed innocuous enough, no more than casual conversation, except the man was a cop. Patsy hesitated.

He glanced her way and she cursed those reflective sunglasses that prevented her from getting a good look at his eyes.

"Don't you know?" he demanded. "What kind of mother leaves home with a sick baby if she doesn't have to?"

Her temper flared and she clutched Billy a little tighter. "He wasn't sick when we left home."

"When was that?"

"A few days ago," she conceded.

"And the baby's father?"

She'd known the question would come up sooner or later. She'd been praying for later, long enough to have manufactured a believable story. Forced to improvise quickly, she said only, "He's not around."

"I see," Justin said slowly, his expression thoughtful. "You know, if you don't have a place to go, Los Piños isn't a bad little town."

Startled by the suggestion, she stared. "You wouldn't object? Under the circumstances, I was sure you'd want us as far from your town as possible."

He glanced over at her. "You ever stolen anything before?"

"No."

"Why should I believe you?"

"Because it's the truth," she said fiercely. "If it

hadn't been for Billy getting sick, I wouldn't have done it this time. I would have come here, found a place for us to stay, gotten a job. We're looking for a fresh start, Deputy Adams, not trouble and definitely not a handout.''

Even from behind those damnable sunglasses, she could feel his penetrating gaze. It was enough to make a liar squirm. Patsy sat perfectly still and withstood it.

''What's your name?''

''Patsy Gresham,'' she said, resorting to her maiden name. If he checked the car tags, he'd know better, but if not, if luck was on her side, she could preserve the illusion for a little while at least.

He nodded. ''Okay, then, Patsy Gresham. I suppose having you stick around won't be a problem. Just know I'll be keeping an eye on you.''

She could just imagine. He'd probably spread the word from one end of town to the other that Patsy Gresham couldn't be trusted. What kind of life could she make for herself with a cloud of suspicion hanging over her head?

''I won't tell a soul about what happened today, if that's what's worrying you,'' he said, his expression softening as if he'd read her mind and wanted to reassure her. ''You'll move into town with a clean slate.''

''Why are you being so nice?''

Once more, the suggestion that he was anything other than a tough, by-the-book lawman seemed to make him uncomfortable. "Damned if I know," he said eventually. "Just don't make me regret it."

If Patsy had her way, not only wouldn't he regret it, he'd never set eyes on her again. Even in a town the size of Los Piños, it ought to be easy enough to disappear if she wanted to make it happen.

Then she took another long look at the man beside her. Of course, Justin Adams struck her as the kind of stubborn, determined man who could find whomever he set out to find. She'd just have to make darned sure he never had any reason to hunt for her.

Justin was losing it. He knew because there was no way in hell under normal circumstances he would have let a criminal off the way he was letting Patsy Gresham go free, despite what Sharon Lynn wanted.

What was it his cousin had asked? Was it the green eyes or the tears that did it? Neither, he had wanted to shout. Now he wasn't so sure.

Every time he glanced into the woman's sad, wary eyes, he felt some subtle change deep inside him. He wanted to strangle whoever had brought such sorrow into her life. She was entirely too young to look so beaten. And yet there was a surprising strength and feistiness about her. She might be down, but she definitely wasn't out. He found such resilience admirable.

On the way back into town he'd reached a decision. Until he knew more, he wanted Patsy Gresham right where he could keep an eye on her. He could just imagine the kind of razzing he'd take for that. No one in his family would believe for an instant that his motives were altruistic. He could explain from now until every head of Adams cattle was counted that he was being cautious, trying to prevent a more serious crime from taking place, but they wouldn't buy it. Not once they got a look at Patsy, anyway. They'd blame it on his hormones and his good nature and nothing he could say would change their minds.

She was a beautiful woman, all right. Fragile and road weary as she was, there was a delicacy about her that brought a man's protective instincts surging to life. And her mouth, those luscious, sensual lips, well, it was the sort of mouth just made for kissing. Justin's gaze had been drawn to it again and again, wondering what those lips would taste like.

Right. Like he needed to get mixed up with a woman who might be an everyday, common thief. No, what he needed to do was to send Patsy Gresham packing, send her into some other jurisdiction where she'd be another lawman's problem.

The words had been on the tip of his tongue, too. He'd been ready to tell her that the second her car was brought back into town and filled with gas, courtesy of the deputy sheriff, he wanted her gone.

Instead, he'd encouraged her to stay. There were names a whole lot stronger than *fool* for the kind of man that made him. *Jerk* and *idiot* came to mind. It was also pretty clear which part of his anatomy had been doing his thinking.

"Do you have any money at all?" he asked, trying to stay focused.

"No," she admitted after a long hesitation. "At least I won't have any once I buy gas. But I'm willing to work for room and board. I just need a break, that's all. I don't want charity."

To his dismay, he realized what he was going to do the second he crossed into the town limits. A few minutes later he pulled to a stop in front of the house that belonged to his sister, Dani. She still operated her veterinary practice from one side of it, but the living quarters had been empty ever since her marriage. If he asked, Dani would agree in a heartbeat to let Patsy and the baby use the house.

But before taking Patsy Gresham and her baby inside, there were a few more questions he needed answered.

"That car of yours is pretty expensive," he said carefully, watching her intently. "Also, I'm no fashion expert, but I have enough female cousins with expensive taste to know quality when I see it."

Her chin tilted up a notch. "So?"

"The two things combined make me wonder why you appear to be in such dire straits."

"Haven't you heard? Appearances can be deceiving."

"Meaning that those things aren't expensive or meaning that you're not in dire straits? Maybe you didn't need to steal that Tylenol. Maybe you were just doing it for kicks. I've heard there are rich ladies who get their thrills that way."

Indignant color flared in her cheeks. "Of course not. You've seen for yourself. Billy is sick."

"And you don't have the money for the medicine."

"Right."

Her lower lip quivered and she looked as if she were about to cry. Justin really didn't want to deal with a flood of tears, but he had no choice.

"Hand me your purse," he said quietly.

She stared at him. "Why?"

"So I can see for myself what shape you're in financially."

She hugged the white leather bag almost as tightly as she clutched her son. "I don't think so."

"I'm ordering you to."

"And I'm telling you, you'll have to get a search warrant if you want to go poking through my things."

To his regret, she had a point. He had been hoping it wouldn't come to that, that she'd cooperate voluntarily.

"Look, if you'll just get my car back here and loan me the money for some food, I'll buy my own gas with the money I have left and be on my way. I can see that staying here isn't such a good idea. For all the pretty words, Officer, it's clear you don't really trust me."

"If you'd let me take a look in your purse, it would go a long way toward changing that," he cajoled.

"Not a chance," she said, her gaze clashing with his.

Justin debated the meaning of her resistence. She could just be a woman who knew her rights and intended to protect them. Or else she was hiding something. Maybe both. He was going to have to decide quickly whether it would be smarter to encourage her to leave town or to stay right here where he could keep an eye on her until he knew more. He gambled on the latter. It was probably better that he not examine his motives too closely.

"Okay, come with me."

Her gaze narrowed suspiciously. "Where?"

"We're going to talk to my sister Dani about using the other half of this house. It's fully furnished and, other than crashing here occasionally after a late night with an injured animal, she doesn't use it."

There was no mistaking the quick survey she did of the white house with its neat lawn, nor the flaring of hope in her eyes. The house was small and tidy. Something told him it was nothing at all like what she was used to. He waited to see how she'd react.

"Do you really think she'd let me use it for a few days, just until I get on my feet?" she asked eagerly.

Her reaction went a long way toward reassuring him. "If I know Dani, she'll insist on it."

"Maybe you should go ask her first. It'll be easier for her to say no if I'm not standing there with Billy staring her in the face."

Justin grinned. "Which is precisely why I want you to come along. One look at you and the baby and she'll be running out to stock the refrigerator for you. Dani is a very soft touch when it comes to taking in strays. You'll see what I mean when you keep tripping over all the kittens underfoot."

"Kitty?" the boy echoed happily, coming awake again. "Where kitty?"

Justin reached down and took him from his mother's lap. The boy came to him eagerly. Justin grazed his cheek with his knuckles and noted that whatever fever he'd had seemed to have come down. "Inside, son. Want to see?"

His dark eyes regarded Justin somberly, but he nodded at once. "See kitties."

Justin started up the walk, leaving Patsy no choice but to follow.

"Hey, sis, you around here someplace?" Justin called out, striding straight through the crowded waiting room and into the back, where there was a cacophony of sound from the animals being boarded here while families went on summer vacations. A cat promptly wound between his legs, almost tripping him.

"Dani, dammit. Get these cats away from me."

His sister poked her head out of one of the tiny examining rooms. "Justin, why are you raising such a ruckus?" she demanded, then spotted Billy. "Oh, my, isn't he darling? Where'd you find him?"

Justin nodded over his shoulder. "He came with her."

His sister's gaze shifted at once to Patsy. "Ah, yes, I see," she murmured.

Justin regarded her suspiciously. "What does that mean?"

"It means Sharon Lynn mentioned you were hot on the trail of a woman and a baby."

"Sharon Lynn has a big mouth."

"I had to pry it out of her," Dani assured him. "After I'd heard about it from three other people."

Justin sighed. There were no secrets in Los Piños, not when it came to an Adams. "They need a place to stay."

"And you were thinking that they could use this place," she guessed.

He grinned sheepishly. "Well, you're never here. Maybe Patsy could look after the animals for you at night. I'm sure your husband would appreciate having you home all night long for a change."

"An interesting deal." She glanced at Patsy, who was hovering in the doorway. "How do you feel about it?"

Justin waited uneasily. There was no predicting how she would react. Patsy had been surprising him from the second they'd met. So far he'd seen no evidence of uppity, high society ways, but maybe she'd draw the line at caring for a bunch of sick animals. A part of him hoped she would.

In fact, she seemed about to argue, then she glanced his way and sighed. "I'd be grateful," she said with apparent sincerity. "And of course I'd be willing to look after the animals in return, at least until I can get a job and pay you rent."

"No need to worry about that," Dani replied. "We'll try it for a few days and see how it goes." She reached for Patsy's hand. "Come with me. I'll show you around."

Justin would have followed, but Billy patted his cheek. "Want to see kitties," he reminded Justin.

"So you shall," he promised, pausing in the kitchen where several cats were sprawled in patches of sunlight. He hunkered down so Billy could see. The boy's coal black eyes lit up.

"Kitties," he whispered with obvious satisfaction. "Nice kitty?"

Justin nodded and set the boy on his feet. "You can pet them."

Billy toddled to the closest one and bent down until he was practically nose to nose with it. "Kitty," he pronounced, and petted it gently on the head. The cat, used to the comings and goings of Dani's rambunctious stepsons, merely yawned widely and stretched before curling up again with its head resting on its paws.

Billy toddled on unsteady legs toward another and went through the same routine again. Not until he'd greeted every cat in the kitchen did he come back to Justin and hold out his arms to be picked up.

"Mama," he whispered, as if he'd just noticed she was missing. Tears began to well up in his eyes.

"It's okay, fella. Your mama's right here. We'll go find her, okay?"

A thumb went into his mouth and he nodded. "'Kay."

His mother might be all bristly caution, but Billy was so thoroughly trusting it made Justin's heart ache with unexpected longing. He'd never given much thought to marriage and kids. If he wanted to hold a baby, there were plenty to choose from in his family. If he wanted to be surrounded by laughter and love, he could invite himself to dinner at any number of homes.

There was something very different about holding a child that belonged to you, though. He'd seen it in the awed expressions of his cousins' husbands. Something told him that it might feel a whole lot like the sensation rushing over him now.

And that, given how very little he knew about Patsy Gresham and her true circumstances, was a very dangerous reaction.

Chapter Three

Justin saw to it that Patsy Gresham and her baby were settled at Dani's. He made sure her car was filled with gas and parked out front. He even had the Italian restaurant down the block send over dinner.

And then he washed his hands of the entire situation. He'd done his good deed for the week. Maybe even for the whole year. He predicted if word got around that he'd not only let a shoplifter get away, but that he'd taken her under his wing, he'd never hear the end of it.

As it turned out, it didn't take long for word to get around. He was the butt of a fair bit of good-natured teasing from his uncles and cousins at the poker game that night at White Pines. Obviously Sharon Lynn had decided to spill the beans, after all. She must not have taken his threat to have a revealing talk with her fiancé all that seriously.

"Don't pay any attention to them, son," Grandpa Harlan advised, giving him a pat on the shoulder. "They've gotten so old now, they don't recall what it's like to be captivated by a pretty face."

"Except for me, of course," Harlan Patrick said. "I'm younger than Justin."

"And you've never been known to miss a pretty face," Justin retorted. "Is there a woman in this town you haven't chased after at one time or another?"

"Not since I met Laurie," Harlan Patrick said piously. "She'd poke my eyes out if she caught me looking at another woman."

"She just has you thinking she would," Grandpa Harlan corrected. "Laurie is the sweetest little gal you've ever brought around. She has a mighty nice voice, too."

"Yes, indeed," Justin agreed. "One of these days Laurie's going to run off to Nashville and leave Harlan Patrick pining away back here."

His cousin scowled at him. The remark had cut a little too close to Harlan Patrick's greatest fear and Justin knew it.

"How'd we get on my love life, anyway?" Harlan Patrick grumbled. "We were talking about you and the shoplifter."

"Don't call her that," Justin said harshly.

"Why not? Isn't that what you and Sharon Lynn caught her doing?"

"She was desperate," he countered defensively.

"Besides, unless a person's tried and convicted, you shouldn't go throwing names around. She could sue you for slander."

"And probably hire my wife to do it," Grandpa Harlan warned. "Janet would just love to get her teeth into a case like that. She hates being retired from her law practice. One of these days she's going to stir up a mess of trouble, just so she can get herself into the thick of it."

"From what I've seen over the years, Daddy, you're all the trouble Janet can cope with," Justin's Uncle Cody said.

Grandpa Harlan scowled. "Watch your tongue, boy. I'm not too old to throw you out of here. Maybe I'll cut you out of the will while I'm at it. White Pines can skip right past you and go straight to Harlan Patrick."

Cody took the good-humored teasing in stride. "Daddy, you've been threatening to take this ranch from me since I can remember. One of these days I'm going to call you on it. I'll hire Janet to contest the will."

"Can't do it," Grandpa Harlan said triumphantly. "It'd be a conflict of interest."

"Is anybody actually going to play poker tonight?" Justin inquired with a wistful glance at the hand he was holding. "I'm feeling lucky."

Harlan Patrick shot him a knowing look. "I'll just bet you are." He tossed some money into the pot. "Okay, let's see those cards you're so proud of."

"Oh, shut up," Justin muttered, and slapped three

aces on the table to take the pot from his mouthy cousin.

From that moment on, he tolerated the jokes and proceeded to whip their tails. He walked away from the poker table a good deal richer than he had been when he sat down.

What troubled him, though, was the fact that his first instinct was to give some of his winnings to Patsy Gresham to make sure she got by until she could find a real job.

Obviously he was turning soft, which was why half a dozen people got tickets for minor traffic violations before he stopped for breakfast the next morning.

When he saw who was about to start serving up eggs behind the counter at Dolan's, he wished he'd stayed on the street and given out another dozen citations.

Patsy rose at the crack of dawn, still unable to believe her luck. The tiny house Justin had arranged for her to use was perfect for her and Billy. The furnishings were old, but cheerful with all the chintz upholstery. The rooms were bright and airy.

"I could be happy here," she thought as she stretched and pulled on her robe. It was Dani's doing, of course, and not her own, but the house felt like a home. It wasn't as lavish as the one Will had insisted on buying, but it had a warmth and charm that the house in Oklahoma had lacked no matter how hard she'd tried to turn it into a home.

She checked on Billy, then went into the kitchen

where she found cereal, milk and bread, courtesy of Dani, along with a note. "Make yourselves at home. We'll talk later about what you can do to help with the animals. Dani."

A nice woman, she concluded. She'd liked her instantly the day before, just as she'd been drawn to Sharon Lynn at the drugstore. It had been a long time since she'd had girlfriends. Will hadn't encouraged her to have any life at all outside of caring for him and Billy.

Maybe these two women could become real friends in time, she thought wistfully. Maybe there would come a time when she'd be able to confide the truth about her circumstances to them, instead of living this lie. Maybe she could tell them about the fear that had been gnawing at her ever since she'd discovered her husband's violent side.

First, though, she had to make amends to one of them. As soon as she got Billy up and dressed, she postponed breakfast and headed toward the drugstore, determined to get the apology over with. They were there as soon as the doors opened. Relieved that there was no one else around, Patsy faced Sharon Lynn uncertainly.

"I came to apologize and to thank you for not pressing charges," she said. "I would never have done it, not in a million years, if I hadn't been so worried about Billy."

"I know," Sharon Lynn said, and sounded as if she meant it. She also sounded as if that were the last word she intended to say on the subject. "How about some coffee? I could fix some cereal for Billy, if you like.''

Could it possibly be that easy? Patsy thought in wonder. Still chagrined by her uncharacteristic behavior the day before, Patsy started to refuse, but Sharon Lynn was already pouring the coffee and dumping cereal into a bowl.

''Dry or with milk?'' she asked, taking the decision out of Patsy's hands.

''Dry for Billy,'' Patsy said. ''He can eat it with his fingers. Otherwise there's no telling where he's likely to fling it with a spoon.''

Sharon Lynn set the bowl on the counter in front of Billy, then grinned as he grabbed a fistful and shoved it into his mouth.

''His table manners leave something to be desired,'' Patsy apologized ruefully.

''How old is he?''

''He just turned two.''

''Then he's got a few years before people start holding that against him. Besides, once you've been to a family dinner at our place, missile strikes would probably seem tame. There are a lot of kids. We've all been brought up to have endless patience. My grandfather, Harlan Adams, would rather have the chaos than a clean house any day.''

Patsy grinned. ''Maybe he can say that because he's not the one who has to clean it up.''

''Oh, I've seen him on his hands and knees chasing after cornflakes and toys a time or two. Of course, he's in his eighties now and he's not as agile as he once was, but he set a good enough example for his sons that they're pretty decent housekeepers if the need arises. They all married women who see to it the need arises every now and then, just to keep them humble.''

''It must be wonderful to have so much family,'' Patsy said, unable to hide the wistful note in her voice.

''Your own is small?''

''Just me and my parents.''

''And you couldn't go to them for help when things got tough for you and the baby?'' Sharon Lynn asked.

Patsy shook her head. ''No, not this time,'' she said, unable to meet the other woman's gaze for fear all the tears she'd been bottling up would come pouring out.

''I see.'' Sharon Lynn's expression softened. ''I hear Justin arranged for you to stay at Dani's.''

Patsy knew enough about small towns not to be surprised that news had traveled so quickly, especially when it involved family members. ''For the time being anyway.''

Sharon Lynn seemed startled by her reply. ''Why on earth wouldn't you go on staying there? It's a great house. It's small, but surely it's big enough for just you and Billy.''

''Of course it is, and I'm truly grateful to her for letting us move in on such short notice.'' Patsy couldn't say that she was afraid she might have to move on, that her husband would discover her whereabouts and come after her. Instead, she said only,

"But I need a job, and someone to look after Billy. I haven't even had time to check the want ads yet to see if there are any openings here. I can't stay in Los Piños indefinitely without work."

"Then you have work," Sharon Lynn said with no hesitation at all.

Patsy stared at her. "What?"

"You can work right here. I can use the help. The lunch counter's busier than ever and so's the pharmacy. The pharmacist can't keep up with prescriptions and all the gift sales we're making now that I've expanded that section."

She smiled persuasively. "So, what do you think? Want to give it a try? I can pay you a halfway decent salary and you'll get tips when you work the counter. I know Dani's not going to charge an arm and a leg for the house. No one was using it anyway. And you'll be able to eat here, so you won't have grocery expenses."

It was more than Patsy had ever dreamed of when she'd walked through the door a few minutes earlier. Though she'd trained as a secretary, she'd known she wouldn't be able to find work in that field, not without being able to give references, and she surely couldn't list Will's firm on her résumé. This job was ideal. She didn't have to think twice about it. "I'll take it," she said at once.

"You're sure?" Sharon Lynn asked. "I have to warn you, it gets crazy in here sometimes and I'm going off on a one-week honeymoon at the end of the month. You'll be on your own. Can you cook?"

"If you'll go over the menu with me, I can do it," Patsy assured her. She'd worked in a place just like this back home one summer while she was taking her secretarial training. This job would be a breeze. "And I've run a cash register before. I'm sure I'll pick up the rest in no time."

"You don't have to sell me. I made the offer, remember?"

"I wouldn't want you to regret it."

"I won't," Sharon Lynn said with confidence. "When can you start?"

"What about now?" She glanced over at Billy, who was happily mashing cereal on the counter. "Unless you'd rather I make arrangements for him so he's not in the way."

"He's not in the way. If he gets fussy, you can leave and take him home for a nap. Someone over at Dani's will keep an eye on him for you."

Patsy grinned at her enthusiasm and quick solutions to every possible problem Patsy suggested. "You must be really desperate for help."

"Not today, but given the daze I'm in just thinking about everything that's left to do for the wedding, desperation is not far off." Sharon Lynn grinned ruefully and admitted, "And there are any number of people in town who'll be relieved that someone else is going to help with the cooking in here. I've been a bit absentminded lately. It's given the menu some interesting and not entirely successful twists."

Patsy grinned back at her as she climbed off the

stool and started to join Sharon Lynn behind the counter. "What do you want me to do first?"

"Sit back down and eat some breakfast." Before Patsy could protest, Sharon Lynn added, "That's not charity. It's just common sense. You'll be dead on your feet in no time unless you've eaten something. I think scrambled eggs, bacon, hash browns and toast ought to do it," she decided, going to work before Patsy could argue.

Everyone she'd met so far had been so kind Patsy couldn't quite believe her luck. Suddenly she regarded Sharon Lynn suspiciously. "Justin didn't put you up to this, did he?"

"Justin didn't put her up to what?" the very man in question inquired as he came through the door along with a gust of hot, dry air.

"Hiring me," Patsy explained, meeting his gaze for an instant.

For once, with his sunglasses tucked in his pocket, Justin's eyes were visible. She could read the shock registered there. Even though she knew it was justified, it hurt nonetheless.

"Really?" he asked, regarding his cousin warily. "Sharon Lynn, could we talk for a minute?" With a glance in Patsy's direction, he added pointedly, "In the back."

"No, we cannot," Sharon Lynn told him. "I'm busy." She flipped Patsy's eggs on the grill, reached for the toast and buttered it, then placed it all on a plate and slid it in front of Patsy. "Enjoy. The crowd will start coming in in about ten minutes."

Patsy nodded. "I'll be finished."

Justin slid onto the stool next to her. She wondered if he meant to intimidate her, but he merely advised, "If you gulp that down, you'll have indigestion. Sharon Lynn doesn't go light on the grease."

She glanced at him. "Worried about my health all of a sudden?"

"Obviously she's expecting to get a full day's work out of you. I don't want to see her cheated." He regarded her meaningfully.

So, there it was, Patsy thought wearily. The trust he'd promised the day before had barely lasted overnight. She leveled a look straight at him and kept it steady. "I thought you were going to give me an honest chance to start over."

He sighed. "You're right," he conceded grudgingly. "I was."

"Has something changed since last night?"

"He probably had to answer a lot of questions out at White Pines last night at the family poker game," Sharon Lynn chimed in cheerfully. "It's made him edgy."

"I am not edgy," he retorted. "I'm just trying to look out for you. Obviously I'm wasting my time. You think you know it all."

Sharon Lynn grinned at him. "When it comes to Patsy, yes, I do think my judgment's better than yours. After all, I am the one who predicted…"

Justin scowled. "Never mind."

Patsy stared at the two of them, trying to guess

what the unspoken hints were all about. "Predicted what?"

"Nothing," Sharon Lynn soothed. "Justin's just the family worrywart. Why don't you get back here and fix him some scrambled eggs and a couple of pancakes? I'll pour him some nice strong black coffee. That ought to improve his mood."

To Patsy's surprise, he didn't argue. Instead he turned his attention to Billy.

"So, young man, what are you up to over there? Has any of that cereal actually made it into your mouth?"

Billy promptly abandoned the mess he was making and reached for Justin. "Up?" he pleaded.

Patsy envisioned all the goo on Billy's hands being transferred to Justin's starched uniform shirt and winced. "No, baby. I don't think so."

To her amazement, Justin ignored her and accommodated Billy. He scooped him up, apparently oblivious to the mess the baby was bound to make of his clothes. Apparently a whole lot more bonding than she'd been aware of had gone on the day before.

"He's fine where he is. You don't have to do that," she told Justin, eyeing him nervously as Billy patted his cheeks with sticky hands.

"It's not a problem."

"But—"

"I said it's not a problem."

And that, she concluded, was that.

After that, she didn't have time to worry about it. As Sharon Lynn had predicted, the counter began to fill up with regulars eager for a little breakfast and a lot of chitchat over the latest local gossip. Several speculative looks were cast her way. Ignoring them and the gentle banter that ensued, she concentrated on filling orders as quickly as Sharon Lynn passed them to her.

Even though she never once looked back, she was aware of the precise instant that Justin Adams slid off his stool and left. The prickling sensation at the back of her neck vanished and the tension in her shoulders eased.

When the crowd began to thin out, Sharon Lynn introduced her to the handful of remaining customers. At the sight of a burly man in uniform, her nerves jumped.

"This is the sheriff, Tate Owens, Justin's boss. Don't mind the scowl. He looks less fierce once he's had a couple of doughnuts."

"I wish," the man said, casting a longing gaze toward the already depleted display on the counter. "Juice and dry toast for me today. The doc put me on a diet yesterday. He's grumbling about my cholesterol again."

"How about some oatmeal?" Sharon Lynn suggested.

"Not without cream and lots of brown sugar," he lamented. "No, I'll stick with the toast today and some of that blackberry jam, if you have it."

"I keep it back here just for you," Sharon Lynn said.

Patsy noted where Sharon Lynn kept it, so she

could supply it on request if she was here alone. She was about to gather up Billy and slip into the back room for a break, when the sheriff spoke directly to her.

"You're new in town."

She met his gaze evenly, fighting the sick sensation in the pit of her stomach. "Yes. My son and I got here yesterday."

"Didn't take you long to find work," he observed.

"No. Sharon Lynn's been very kind."

He nodded. "Welcome to Los Piños, then. You run into any problems, let me know."

The offer was made with such absolute sincerity that for a fleeting instant Patsy had the absurd desire to unburden herself to this man. Who knew, maybe she'd be lucky one more time and he would see what she'd been up against. Maybe he could protect her from Will. She sighed with regret. She couldn't take a chance that it would go the other way.

Instead, she smiled noncommittally. "Thanks. I'll remember that."

"You're from Oklahoma," he noted conversationally. "What part?"

She named her old hometown, rather than Oklahoma City. "I doubt you've ever heard of it. It's tiny, not even as big as Los Piños."

"Must be," he said, his expression thoughtful. "I grew up around Oklahoma City myself and I never heard of it. Of course, my memory's not what it used to be, either. Haven't been home in years, not since my folks died about ten years back."

When he'd mentioned Oklahoma City, Patsy's heart had slammed against her ribs. It hadn't eased back into a normal rhythm until he'd said how long it had been since he'd been back.

Ten years ago Will had been just starting law school. His face—and hers—hadn't been on the front pages of the local papers until much more recently. She doubted that a mayor's race in Oklahoma City would make the local paper here in Los Piños.

"Do you still stay in touch with old friends?" she asked carefully.

"Nope. My friends and family are here now. Haven't heard from a soul back that way. Skipped my high school reunions. Couldn't think of what I'd have to say to people I hadn't seen in years."

"Too bad," she said, though the relief that washed over her said just the opposite. "It's always sad when we lose touch with old friends."

"What about you? You still have family there?"

"Some," she said.

Thankfully, he let it go at that. Much more poking and prodding, no matter how innocently intended, and she was pretty sure she would have cracked. She just wasn't cut out for this much deception. It was a habit that had started when she and Will were first dating and trying to keep it a secret from their co-workers. She'd been lousy at it then, too. Their relationship had been discovered in no time, which was one reason they'd married in such haste. Will had wanted to quiet the gossip.

Tate Owens drew her attention again. "We'll have

to compare notes sometime. It's been my experience that it's a mighty small world. Maybe we'll know some folks in common.''

''I doubt that,'' she said. ''Like I said, the town where I grew up was really small.''

He nodded. ''Okay. Well, I'd better get out of here. If I don't stay on my toes, Justin's going to steal my job right out from under me.''

''As if he would ever try,'' Sharon Lynn chided. ''You were his mentor, Tate. And everybody knows you're the best sheriff ever. You'll stay in the job as long as you want it. Besides, something tells me half the town is going to be mad as heck at him this morning.''

Tate Owens moaned. ''What's he done now?'' he asked in a resigned tone.

''Last time I saw him, he was handing out parking tickets all up and down Main Street.''

''Damn, I thought I'd broke him of that. The town doesn't need the money, and I don't need the aggravation.'' He slapped his Stetson on his head and walked out the door.

Patsy watched him go, then turned to Sharon Lynn. ''What's with the parking tickets?''

''Tate tends to ignore minor infractions like that. He thought the parking meters were a nuisance in the first place. Justin goes crazy every once in a while and starts handing out tickets. Tate spends the rest of the day soothing ruffled feathers.''

Patsy shook her head. ''I don't get it. If the people are breaking the law, shouldn't they get tickets?''

"Technically, yes. And Justin is a by-the-book kind of man, especially after he's done something that makes him worry whether he's listening too much to his heart," she said with a look in Patsy's direction.

"Am I supposed to understand that?"

"You're here, aren't you?"

"Yes," she said, still confused.

"And not in a jail cell."

"Oh."

Sharon Lynn grinned. "Oh, indeed. Bottom line, it's my guess that you're the one behind today's rampage with the parking tickets."

Patsy would have chuckled if she hadn't been able to imagine what everyone in town would have to say if they knew to blame her.

Sharon Lynn's expression turned thoughtful. "Something tells me you're going to be good for him," she said quietly.

"Me? I don't think so," Patsy said at once. If Justin Adams knew the truth about her, he probably wouldn't even blink before tossing her in that jail cell and throwing away the key.

Chapter Four

While Justin had been thoroughly disconcerted by the sight of Patsy Gresham working at Sharon Lynn's that morning, he told himself he'd merely found it troubling that she was becoming so intimately entwined with his family.

What really worried him more, was that quick little shiver of awareness he'd felt when he spotted her. He knew his hormones well enough to recognize a man-woman thing when he felt it, and it was the very last reaction he ought to be having to the woman, not with all those legitimate suspicions he couldn't quite dismiss.

Except for a minor fender bender in midafternoon, the rest of the day had been uneventful. It had taken all of his willpower to keep from wandering into Dolan's a few more times to make sure Patsy's hand wasn't in the till or anywhere else it didn't belong. His conscience had reminded him that he'd promised her an honest chance.

By nightfall, though, he couldn't battle his desire to see how she'd fared. The fact that he chose to get his answers from her, rather than from Sharon Lynn, meant nothing, he assured himself. After all, Patsy was right here in town, while Sharon Lynn was all the way out at the ranch. It was pure logic and convenience that sent him to her doorstep.

Yeah, right.

Dusk was falling by the time he'd showered and changed into jeans and a T-shirt. He strolled up the walkway at Dani's with his mind on the excuse he was going to have to come up with for his visit.

He was about to knock on the front door, when he heard chaos erupt in the veterinary clinic. Muttering under his breath about the fact that he'd left his gun at home, he raced around to the clinic entrance and pounded on the door. It was opened by a frazzled Patsy, backed up by a snarling dog that looked perfectly capable of tearing both of them limb from limb.

"Oh, it's you," she said, and turned back toward the dog, which was straining on its leash. "Punk, hush up. You'll get your food when it's your turn."

Her total lack of concern about the huge dog's barking brought a smile to Justin's lips. He leaned back against the doorway and admired the methodical way she was moving from pen to pen.

"If I were you, I'd take care of Punk first before

he decides to turn you into dinner,'' he observed casually.

She shot him a defiant look that would have been wasted on Punk. "And let him win? I don't think so. He's nothing but a big bully. He'll wait his turn."

Even though she spoke with conviction, he noticed that she skirted carefully just out of the huge dog's reach as she worked. He also noticed that her hands were trembling as she scooped food into the other animals' dishes. Obviously this was some sort of test she was putting herself through. Was it possible that Punk represented another bully in Patsy's life? Perhaps one she hadn't stood up against? Justin couldn't help wondering about all the gaps in her background he hadn't been able to fill in.

"What are you doing here?" she asked as she kept on working.

"I just thought I'd stop by to see how your first day on the job at Dolan's had gone."

A smile broke across her face. "It went great. Everyone is really nice. They were very patient."

"It didn't seem to me they needed much patience. You were a whiz at the grill when I was there, better than Sharon Lynn, in fact. Have you done that sort of work before?"

"Way back," she admitted.

He grinned. "It couldn't have been that long ago. You can't be more than what? Maybe nineteen?"

"Twenty-three, actually." She turned a knowing look on him. "Probing for information again, Deputy?"

He shook his head. "Just making conversation."

"If you don't have anything better to do, maybe you could take Punk for a walk. He could use the exercise."

Justin regarded the dog warily. "You have to take him for a walk? Is Dani crazy?"

She grinned at him. "Don't tell me you're scared of a little ole dog."

"That dog is bigger than I am. He does not have a friendly demeanor."

"He still needs to be walked."

Justin sighed. He knew perfectly well he couldn't go off and leave her to handle the beast. When they found itsy-bitsy pieces of her the next morning, he'd never forgive himself.

"I'll walk him," he agreed grudgingly, "if you'll get Billy and come with me. We'll stop for ice cream."

He could read the temptation in her eyes. How long had it been since she'd had such a simple pleasure, he wondered. How long since her son had been given any kind of treat at all? With money scarce, he doubted there had been many. Patsy struck him as a very practical sort of woman who would put the basics first.

"Where?" she asked cautiously. "Dolan's is closed and I haven't seen any other places for ice cream around town."

He grinned. "But I know the owner at Dolan's and I have a spare key for emergencies."

"Somehow I doubt this qualifies as an emergency."

"True," he agreed. "Actually, though, I wasn't thinking of Dolan's. I just bought a half gallon of rocky road and some cones. I figured we could stop by my place. It's only a few blocks from here."

That all-too-familiar wary expression clouded her eyes. "I don't know."

"Is Billy asleep?"

"No. He's surrounded by kitties and glued to a video Dani left for him. It's one of his favorites. I doubt we'll be able to pry him away from the TV."

"Sure we can. Besides he should get out and get some fresh air, too. A walk will be good for all of us."

"Obviously, you haven't done much walking with a two-year-old. One of us will be carrying him before we get home."

"I can carry him."

"And control Punk?"

"That, too. Consider it a challenge."

Her eyes sparkled at that. It appeared he'd finally made the offer too tempting to resist.

"In that case, I'll get Billy. You're in charge of Punk."

He eyed the beast and wondered if it was too late to reconsider. "Okay," he said, approaching the dog cautiously. "Come on, boy. Let's go for a walk."

Apparently that was the magic word. The dog began pulling at his restraint and barking joyously. As Justin neared, Punk jumped up and put both paws on

Justin's shoulders and began trying to lick him to death. Justin managed to pull back just enough to glance at Patsy, who was grinning from ear to ear.

"You knew, didn't you?"

"Dani did mention he really, really liked to walk."

"And that he was a pussycat underneath all that snarling?" he questioned.

"That, too, but I wasn't sure I could believe her on that point."

"So I was the human guinea pig?"

"Something like that."

Justin frowned at her as the dog slobbered all down the front of him. "You'll pay for this, darlin'. I guarantee it."

Even in the face of his threat, she chuckled. "Sorry. I can't help it. You look so…"

"So what?"

"Surprised," she suggested. "Indignant."

"Wait till you see me when I'm flat-out furious," he warned.

Her grin never faltered. "You're forgetting something, Deputy. I've been there, done that."

Justin paused. So she had. And surprisingly, despite the wariness he'd read in her eyes, despite a momentary panic, she hadn't run for cover. Something told him, though, that they might both be better off if she had. There were secrets with this woman, secrets and lies. He didn't doubt it for an instant. When the truth finally came out, which of them was going to be the one most hurt by it?

* * *

Every instinct she possessed told Patsy to avoid Justin Adams and yet, when he'd proposed helping her to walk that huge dog and getting ice cream, she hadn't been able to resist. For Billy's sake, she reassured herself. It had been a long time since Billy had an innocent outing, an even longer time since he'd had one with an adult male who actually seemed to enjoy his company.

Will hadn't been the kind of father who carted a messy child off for ice cream unless there was a photo opportunity in it for him. Then the ice cream had been little more than a prop and Billy had been handed back to her the instant the cameras were out of range.

In the living quarters beside the clinic, she'd had only to mention ice cream and Billy had toddled toward her with his arms upstretched.

"Go," he pleaded, the video forgotten. "Go now."

"We'll go now, but you have to walk. I'm not going to carry you, okay?"

"'Kay," he agreed, his head bobbing. "Big boy."

She grinned at him. "Yes, you are my big boy." And the treasure of her life. Everything she was doing, the risk she was taking, starting over in a new place, all of it was for him. She wouldn't have been able to bear it if he'd been injured—even accidentally—in the cross fire between her and Will.

Justin stuck his head into the room. "All set?"

At the sight of him, Billy ran straight toward him on unsteady legs. "Hi, ya."

"Hi, yourself."

"We go for ice cream," Billy announced.

"I know."

"You, too?"

"Yep, me, too."

"Mama, Justin go, too."

"That's right, baby."

Billy raced for the clinic and passed Punk as if he weren't even there. "Le's go, Mama."

"I'm coming," she assured him. She glanced at Justin. "Are you bringing Punk?"

"Do I have a choice?" he muttered as the dog leaped on him and licked his face. "Down, you beast."

The look of stunned amazement on his face when Punk dutifully sat was priceless. "Dani also mentioned he's very obedient," she said.

"You could have told me that sooner," he grumbled as he headed for the door with the dog heeling on command.

"I wasn't sure I believed her. I figured I'd let you put it to the test."

Justin tightened his hold on the leash and both of them watched with bated breath as Billy marched up to Punk and petted him gently on the nose. "Nice dog."

Punk responded by wagging his tail so hard he shook all over, but he did nothing at all to intimidate his pint-size admirer.

As they started down the block, they passed other families out for an evening stroll. Justin spoke to everyone, but to Patsy's relief he didn't pause to introduce her. Deceiving a handful of people was hard enough. She wasn't ready to put herself to the test with everyone else in town just yet.

Being with Justin like this felt so normal, so ordinary, she couldn't believe it. This was what she'd envisioned her marriage being, the kind of life she'd anticipated with Will. That it had turned out so very differently saddened her more than she could say.

"Hey," Justin said softly. "You okay?"

"Just thinking."

"About?"

"This and that," she equivocated.

"Which made you so sad? This or that?" he inquired lightly.

"What makes you think either one made me sad?"

"There are tears in your eyes."

And now they were spilling down her cheeks, she realized with embarrassment. She brushed them away and forced a smile. "Every now and then I get lost in what might have been."

He regarded her with a troubled expression. "And what might have been makes you sad?"

"No sadder than what was," she admitted and walked quickly on ahead.

"Patsy."

His voice was soft, but something in it commanded her to stop. She hesitated, fought against a fresh batch of tears, then turned back.

"If something's bothering you, you can talk to me. In my line of work, there's not much I haven't seen or heard."

She looked into worried blue eyes and saw the sincere desire to help. As she had said to Tate Owens earlier, she repeated, "Thank you. I'll remember that."

"Something tells me you won't."

"I said I would, didn't I?" she snapped defensively.

"Do you always keep your promises?"

She remembered other promises—vows—she'd made and broken by running off. "When I can," she said quietly.

"What would it take to make you break a promise?" he asked.

"Betrayal," she said without thinking.

There was a quick flash of understanding in his eyes. "Who betrayed you, Patsy?"

"No one," she said hurriedly. "Forget I said that."

His gaze searched her face. She could see there were a hundred questions on the tip of his tongue, but he finally nodded. "For now," he agreed.

Patsy should have felt relieved, but instead the reprieve promised only a temporary solution. Sooner or later, Justin Adams was going to pursue his questioning until he had all the answers he wanted. He was too good a lawman not to. She knew he didn't totally believe a word out of her mouth.

Still she could enjoy tonight. The summer air was dry and stirred by a faint, cooling breeze. The streets of Los Piños were peaceful. The only arguments were between children squabbling over a toy or a game of hopscotch. If there were more serious fights between grown-ups, they were behind closed doors and they weren't her fights. Will Longhorn was far away and, hopefully, nowhere close to finding her. Right this minute she and Billy were safe. They had found a temporary haven, where they could get back on their feet again, where she could rebuild her self-respect.

And even though he represented a very real threat of discovery, Justin Adams also reassured her. She sensed that his quiet strength would never be used against her and, after so many months of fearing for her own safety and Billy's, that was wonderful.

Yet she couldn't help wondering what would happen if Justin knew the truth. Would he feel betrayed because he'd risked believing in her? Would he send her straight back to her husband? Would be believe the lies that Will was bound to tell to discredit her?

Or, as he had with the incident over the Tylenol, would Justin understand that she was only doing what she'd had to do? Would he protect her? Did she even have the right to expect that of him?

As a lawman, yes. It was his sworn duty to keep her safe. Thanks to Sharon Lynn and Tate Owens, she already knew how Justin felt about duty.

But as a man? In less than forty-eight hours she had come to see him as both. Wrong as it was, she had wished, however fleetingly, that she could be loved by a man like Justin Adams. She'd dismissed the thought as ridiculous and hypothetical, not a serious yearning for this particular man. But now, with him beside her, she wondered if the thought had been hypothetical at all, or truly wistful longing?

Forget it, she told herself. It wasn't even something

she could afford to consider until she did something about her marital status. At some point, she would have to file for divorce she supposed, but that meant facing Will, dealing with him in a courtroom at the very least. Now she was too fearful of the outcome to risk it. She would live the rest of her life in limbo if she had to.

"Patsy." Justin spoke quietly as if he feared startling her.

Startled anyway, she jerked, then gazed up into those vivid blue eyes again. "Yes?"

His smile was slow and a little sad, perhaps regretful over frightening her. "We're here."

She glanced toward the neatly tended house, a low brick rambler with roses in the yard and a sheriff's car parked in the driveway. The latter was a shock, a reminder that she'd been too ready to drop her guard.

He led the way inside. Punk was eager to explore, but a soft command to stay had him flopping on the cool marble floor in the foyer.

"The kitchen's this way," Justin said, leading her through a dining room that was empty of furniture.

He spotted her quick look around, then shrugged sheepishly. "I can't decide if I want to use it for a dining room or a family room," he explained. "It seems a little silly to put a fancy table in here, when I never entertain."

He opened a swinging door and gestured inside. "The kitchen's plenty big enough for a table and chairs. Everybody hangs out in here anyway."

Patsy could see why. The antique oak table was

huge and it was surrounded by oak chairs with bright cushions on the seats that matched the curtains hanging at the windows. It was a woman's touch and she wondered with a twinge of jealousy who'd been responsible. The appliances appeared to be brand-new, including a state-of-the-art refrigerator that looked big enough to stock a month's supply of food for a family of eight.

When Justin opened the humongous freezer, she had to laugh. Inside there were two half-gallons of ice cream and nothing else, except perhaps some unseen cubes of ice in the automatic ice maker.

"Kind of a waste of space, isn't it?" she teased.

He shrugged. "I eat out a lot."

"Is the other side any better?"

"See for yourself," he said, opening the door to reveal a couple of cans of soda, some sandwich meat, a loaf of bread, a bottle of ketchup, a jar of mayonnaise, and a stick of butter still in its wrapper.

"Interesting diet you have."

"I eat breakfast at Dolan's, lunch wherever it's convenient and dinner with my folks or Grandpa Harlan. This stuff is good enough for a late-night snack or an emergency lunch on my day off."

"No lady friends to cook for you?" she inquired, all too aware of yet another odd little twinge of envy that came automatically with the question.

"Once in a while," he conceded. "No one special."

She could believe it. She could also believe that he didn't entertain them here. The bare necessities weren't meant to impress anyone. And any woman with marriage on her mind would have long since added her own touches to the room and seen to it that the refrigerator was stocked with tempting dishes meant to win his heart. She wouldn't have stopped with the cushions and matching curtains.

Nope, Patsy concluded, this was the home of a dedicated, unattached bachelor, all right. She found that oddly comforting.

"Ice cream," Billy demanded.

Justin hoisted him up and settled him on the counter, then reached into a cupboard and brought out a box of sugar cones. "One scoop or two?" he inquired, the question directed at Billy, but his unsettling gaze fixed on Patsy.

"One," she insisted, overriding Billy's demand for two. "And prepare for disaster. We probably ought to eat them outside."

"We can take them onto the patio," he said, scooping the rocky road into the cones and handing two to her. When he'd put the carton of ice cream back into the freezer, he picked Billy up and opened the back door to a brick patio and a medium-sized pool that sparkled with underwater lights. Billy clapped his hands in delight.

"Swim, Mama."

"Not now, baby."

She caught Justin's surprised expression.

"He can swim?"

She nodded. "Like a little fish. He had lessons a few months ago. He loves the water." Lessons had been a necessity with the huge pool in their backyard. Even so, she had had safety locks installed on all the doors leading outside to keep Billy from wandering out unattended, lured by the water and oblivious to the potential dangers.

"You'll have to come over sometime and use the pool," Justin said.

"We'll see."

She could see that there were more questions he wanted to ask, such as how a woman who'd been unable to pay for children's Tylenol had afforded swimming lessons or had even had access to a pool. He was probably noting that, right alongside the expensive clothes he'd already commented on and the fancy car, and coming up with a background for her that didn't add up.

"One of these days we're going to have to talk about this," he said, his gaze never leaving hers.

The comment confirmed her worst fears. Patsy sighed and nodded. "One of these days," she conceded.

He nodded slowly, accepting that for now. A plaintive *woof* from inside broke the tension and had them laughing.

"Apparently Punk is tired of being obedient," she noted.

"Should I let him join us or should we head back?"

"We'd better get back," she said reluctantly. "Billy needs to get to sleep. And I have to be up early to get to work."

He gestured behind her. "I don't think Billy's rest is an issue."

She turned and found Billy curled up on a chaise longue sound asleep, his half-eaten ice cream cone melting beside him. Panic spiraled through her at the sight of the mess.

"Oh, dear," she murmured, jumping up at once. "I'll clean it up."

"Stay where you are," he said. "I'll take care of it."

"But—"

"Patsy, it's not a problem. The fabric's washable. Even if it weren't, what would it matter?"

She thought of Will's quick, explosive anger over such minor accidents and wondered at this man who seemed to take the same thing in stride. "Are you sure?" she asked, unable to keep the uneasiness out of her voice.

"Of course, I'm sure," he said, his gaze intent and filled with unspoken curiosity. "Relax. I'll be right back."

Patsy couldn't relax, but she did manage to stay where she was and let Justin deal with the melted ice cream. When it was cleaned up, he hefted Billy into his arms.

"Let's get this guy home and into bed." He glanced at her. "Can you handle Punk?"

"Sure," she said with sheer bravado.

The dog seemed to sense her uncertainty and tested her immediately, but one sharp command from Justin had him behaving.

Back at Dani's Justin took the baby into the bedroom and settled him, then walked back to the front door. He lifted his hand to graze her cheek with his knuckles. Longing shimmered through her, a deep yearning for more than that gentle touch. For now, though—perhaps forever—more was forbidden.

"Thank you," she said, fighting the breathless note in her voice. "I enjoyed the walk and the ice cream."

In fact, she had enjoyed the whole evening entirely too much. It had relaxed her guard around this man. It had made her want things that couldn't be. It would not do to repeat occasions like this too often, for both their sakes.

"We'll have to do it again sometime," he said.

"Sure," she said, but she knew she would have to fight the next invitation.

Tonight had proved beyond any doubt that being around Justin Adams was dangerous. One day soon he wouldn't settle for evasive answers. One day soon he wouldn't settle for the quick brush of his fingertips along her cheek, as he was doing now.

Worse, one day soon, she wouldn't, either. And that could be her downfall.

Chapter Five

Justin had a long and restless night after leaving Patsy. He'd lain awake most of it reciting all the reasons he ought to be fighting his attraction to her for all he was worth. Every instinct he possessed warned him away.

Even without the circumstances of their first meeting still fresh in his mind, he would have known that there were troubling aspects to Patsy Gresham's past. She was too leery of any questions, too skittish around him. He'd noted her easygoing manner with most of the customers in Dolan's the day before and concluded that her nervousness was directed at him. More likely, at his uniform.

There were a couple of obvious reasons for people to be afraid of a cop. Either they'd committed a crime, or they were trying to hide from someone and feared discovery. He wanted to believe it was the latter in Patsy's case.

But who? And why? He wasn't sure he was going to be thrilled with the answers to those questions, either. That probably explained why he hadn't asked them the night before. If he discovered something in Patsy's background that required reporting, he would be duty-bound to deal with it. For the moment, it seemed to him it might be better not to know.

Looking the other way was totally out of character for him. That he was even in such a position was irritating as the dickens. He left for work in a foul humor, which didn't improve when he walked through the door to be greeted by more questions about Patsy.

"Justin, how much do you know about the Gresham woman?" Tate Owens asked before he'd even had time for a decent cup of coffee.

As riled as he was by the question, Justin had anticipated it. He'd known the sheriff wouldn't let the matter rest ever since Tate had come back from Dolan's the day before. He'd found his conversation with Patsy worrisome. "The woman's in some kind of trouble," he'd said then. "I can feel it in my gut."

Justin hadn't been able to argue with him.

"Justin," Tate prodded now. "What do you know about her?"

"Enough," he said curtly.

"Did you run the tag number?"

"No."

"You're sure it's her car?"

If Justin had been the kind of man who squirmed under pressure, he'd have been doing it now. He knew he should have run the check, but he wasn't sure he wanted the answers it might yield. He hadn't even demanded to see the registration.

"Sure enough," he said curtly.

"I don't suppose you checked the registration, either, did you?"

He scowled at Tate. "No, but—"

The sheriff stared at him. "Justin, you're a better cop than that. The woman shows up here out of the blue, tries to steal from your cousin, and you ignore the obvious way to get a clear picture of what we're dealing with? Why?" Tate studied him closely. "Damn, you've got a thing for her, haven't you?"

"Don't be ridiculous."

"Then give me one good reason for not checking her out."

"I did check. I ran through the stolen vehicle reports," he conceded finally. He'd done even that much reluctantly, praying that he wouldn't find a report on a fancy Oklahoma car in the stack.

Tate was only slightly mollified. "Anything there?"

"Nothing."

"You've spent more time with her than I have. What do you think?"

"I think she's trying her best to start over. Maybe we ought to back off and let her."

"What if whatever trouble she's in follows her here

to Los Piños?'' Tate inquired. ''We should be prepared for it, don't you think? We can't help her, if we don't know what to be on the lookout for.''

Justin sighed. He had no argument with his boss's thinking. In law enforcement, especially in a small town with limited resources, it was always better to be prepared.

''We need some answers, son. You know we do.''

''I know. I'll see what I can do.''

''Don't take too long. Every instinct tells me that it won't be long before all hell breaks loose. A classy woman with a baby and a fancy car, but no money...'' He shook his head. ''It has all the earmarks of a woman on the run from her husband.''

Hearing his own suspicion put into words made Justin's heart sink. Every time a voice in his head had started to shout the possibility, he'd tuned out, refusing to listen. He'd looked for a wedding ring, but she hadn't been wearing one. He'd wanted to believe that meant there was no husband. He was smart enough to know better. Rings would be the first thing she'd hide—or hock.

''Any sign she'd been abused?'' Tate asked.

''No bruises, if that's what you mean.'' He had checked, surreptitiously studying every visible inch of her for fading marks on her pale skin. He'd been relieved by the absence of evidence. ''That doesn't mean she wasn't, though.''

He thought of the way she'd reacted to Billy's accident with the ice cream the night before. She'd been too quick to leap to her feet, too panicked over such a trivial incident.

"What about the boy?" Tate inquired just as the same thought struck Justin.

"By God, I hope not," he said tightly, consumed with fury at the slightest possibility that that was the explanation for Patsy being on the run. The one good sign was that Billy had shown no fear at all of him. If he'd been harmed by his father, wouldn't he have been wary of men? He clung to that tiny shred of reassurance.

Tate cleared his throat and regarded Justin uneasily. "Son, are you sure you're the best person to be checking into this. Maybe I ought to look into it myself."

"Why?"

"Could be you're too personally involved."

"Involved? I just met the woman."

"Ever heard about lightning bolts?" the sheriff questioned. "They strike without warning. Only takes an instant to change everything."

Justin thought of the way Patsy's skin had felt under his touch the night before, of the way her soft cheek had warmed, of the flicker of desire he'd been so sure he'd seen in her eyes. And then he considered how badly his body had ached the rest of the night with wanting her, with wanting more than that gentle, fleeting brush of skin against skin.

It meant nothing, he assured himself. Just a natural, hormonal reaction to a beautiful woman's proximity.

"My objectivity's not compromised," he insisted,

partly because he believed it, mostly because he didn't dare consider the possibility that it could be.

Tate's gaze met his and remained steady. Finally he nodded, accepting Justin's word. "If that changes, let me know. You don't just owe it to me. You owe it to her."

"I will," he promised. If the time ever came when he couldn't do his job, surely he would know it, surely he would do the right thing. He wouldn't let pride and pure cussedness stand in his way.

If he did, if it ever came to that, he would have to reexamine exactly who Justin Adams really was, if he really was the honorable, natural born lawman he'd always thought himself to be. Or if he was like any other man who'd bend the rules when they no longer suited him.

The vivacious woman with the sculpted cheekbones and short black hair beckoned to Patsy, then glanced around furtively.

"Where's Sharon Lynn?" she demanded in a hushed voice.

"She went out to run an errand," Patsy said, dropping her own voice to a whisper in response.

The woman's smile was relieved. "Great. Then we can talk. I'm Jenny, Sharon Lynn's stepaunt technically, but that's neither here nor there. Dani should be here any minute. We're planning a surprise bridal shower for Sharon Lynn tomorrow. Can you help?"

Patsy grinned, delighted to be asked to be in on the surprise. "Of course. What do you need me to do?"

"Get her there."

"Where? And how on earth can I get her to go anywhere?"

"Well, that's the beauty of it. We thought we'd have it at your place. I understand you've moved into Dani's old house. Sharon Lynn will never suspect that. Maybe you could invite her to dinner or something. We're going to have it right after she closes up here."

Patsy thought about it. "I suppose I could manage that. I owe her a lot for giving me this job. I'll tell her I want to repay her by having her over for dinner."

"That's perfect. Do you mind us having it there? I suppose I should have asked that first thing, but we were already planning it for Dani's and now you're there, so it didn't seem to make sense to move it. In fact, it works out even better this way, if you don't mind, that is."

"Of course not. The house is Dani's, after all. She's been wonderful about letting me and Billy stay there."

"You're invited, of course. No need to bring a present. Sharon Lynn won't expect it."

"You don't need to include me. I'll lure her over and then Billy and I can just go out to eat."

"Absolutely not. Besides, if you're the one dragging her over there, you can't turn right around and leave. And we all want to get to know you better. Seven o'clock, okay? We'll take care of everything."

"I'll have her there," Patsy promised, already

looking forward to the chance to pay Sharon Lynn back for her kindness by helping with this surprise.

"Terrific. Dani said we could count on you. Got to run. I'm overdue at home and my husband tends to get restless, especially now that I'm pregnant."

She was out the door before Patsy could blink, another whirlwind Adams entering into her life and drawing her into the family circle.

Weighed down by the assignment just given to her, she was a nervous wreck until Sharon Lynn returned.

Forcing a casual note into her voice, she asked, "Sharon Lynn, do you have plans for tomorrow night?"

A frown of concentration knit her brow. "I don't think so, but let me check my calendar. I can't trust myself to remember anything these days. Why?"

"I'd like to have you over for dinner after we close. Nothing fancy, but I really want to do something special to thank you for being so nice to Billy and me. I know you won't have a spare second once all the wedding plans kick into gear."

"Oh, sweetie, that's not necessary. All I did was give you a job and work you to death."

"But after what happened the first time I came in here, a lot of people wouldn't have been so understanding."

"You've more than made up for that. You've only been here two days and already I can't imagine what I ever did without you. You're fitting right in."

Patsy warmed under the heartfelt praise. It had been a long time since anyone had complimented her.

Will's constant carping had eaten away at her self-confidence, eroding it to the point that she hadn't been sure if there was a single thing she could do right at all.

"All I'm doing is scrambling eggs and frying hamburgers," she said quietly.

"It's a lot more than that," Sharon Lynn insisted. "The customers around here can be stingy with praise, but they already love you."

To Patsy's embarrassment, she could feel tears stinging her eyes. "Stop. You're going to make me cry."

Sharon Lynn stared at her. "Just because I'm pointing out the obvious, that you're good at what you do?"

Patsy nodded. "Please," she begged. "Don't ask me to explain."

"I won't," Sharon Lynn agreed, her expression turning fierce. "But if some man has made you feel worthless, then shame on him." She drew in a deep breath, then said more quietly, "If you ever need to talk, I'm a good listener." She gave Patsy a pointed look. "So's Justin."

"I know," Patsy responded. "But there's nothing to talk about."

Sharon Lynn seemed about to argue, then she let it go. "About dinner tomorrow night, if the invitation's still open, I would love to come."

Mission accomplished, Patsy thought triumphantly, pushing aside all other thoughts to focus on tomorrow's surprise. "About seven, right after we close?"

"That will be perfect."

"What will be perfect?" Justin demanded, walking up to settle on a stool at the counter.

He had a worrisome way of sneaking up on her that constantly caught her off guard. One of these days would he overhear something that would give her away?

"Patsy's invited me to dinner tomorrow night," Sharon Lynn explained.

He glanced at her. "Is that so? What about me?"

Patsy shook her head. "Sorry. It's a girls-only night."

"Then maybe I should pick Billy up and take him out for spaghetti with the guys."

The thought of being separated even for a short time from her son panicked her. "No, really, he'll be fine with us," Patsy said at once.

"Maybe it would be fun for Billy," Sharon Lynn said. "Justin's really good with kids."

"I know that. It's just that..." It was just that she envisioned Will coming to claim him when she wasn't around to prevent it. How could she explain that?

"I'll take good care of him," Justin promised. His gaze locked with hers. "No harm will come to him while he's with me."

It was almost as if he knew, she thought, studying his expression for some clue that would tell her if he'd discovered the truth.

She thought of the real purpose for tomorrow's invitation to Sharon Lynn. The house would be crawl-

ing with other women for the shower. It really was
no place for a small child. And surely the safest place
in the world for Billy to be was with a deputy sheriff.

"Okay," she said at last. "Billy loves spaghetti.
Just be aware that he tends to get most of it all over
himself and anyone else who's in his path."

Justin grinned. "In that case, maybe I'll invite Harlan Patrick along."

Sharon Lynn laughed.

"Who's Harlan Patrick?" Patsy asked, watching
their shared amusement and the conspiratorial wink
they exchanged.

"My brother," she explained. "When he's not
herding cattle or up to his elbows in muck, he con-
siders himself quite a fashion plate. There's nothing
Harlan Patrick likes more than a fancy new outfit
that'll impress the ladies. Justin's just imagining how
he'd love to have spaghetti spattered all over his best
western shirt, especially since his girlfriend will be
singing over at the restaurant tomorrow."

"But that's…" Words failed her.

"Dastardly," Sharon Lynn provided.

"Just plain mean," Patsy said.

"Payback," Justin corrected. "Harlan Patrick and
I have a score to settle."

"And you intend to use my son to do it?"

"He and my brother always have a score to settle,"
Sharon Lynn said. "Goodness knows what it's about
this time. Don't worry about it. Just leave them to it.
When Harlan Patrick decides to get even, he won't

take it out on Billy. All his ire will be directed straight back at Justin.''

The idea that a family could engage in teasing and pranks without rancor was so totally alien to the way Patsy had spent the past couple of years that she was enthralled by it. She would almost rather watch Justin get even with his cousin than go through with her role in Sharon Lynn's surprise.

But it was all part of the same cloth, she realized with a sense of wonder. This was a tight-knit, supportive family, the kind she'd always dreamed of being a part of.

"Do you two have any idea how lucky you are?" she asked.

"Of course we do," Sharon Lynn said, clearly grasping her meaning at once. She gave Patsy a tight hug. "You'll see," she promised, glancing toward Justin. "Won't she?"

His gaze caught Patsy's and held. "If I have anything to say about it."

Patsy trembled under the intensity of that look. A fierce longing for what these Adams cousins took for granted rushed over her. Gazing into Justin's eyes she saw what might have been a bold commitment, a promise that was there for the taking if only she could.

If only she could.

She sighed heavily and turned away, busying herself with the last of the day's dishes, which had to be stacked and ready for the morning rush. When she turned again, she realized that Sharon Lynn had silently left, leaving her alone with Justin.

"Come to dinner with me," he suggested. "And before you start making excuses, I've already checked with Dani. She's going to be late at the clinic. She'll look after Billy for another couple of hours. She says he's having the time of his life with the animals. Her boys will be over there soon, too. Billy will be in heaven with all that attention."

"But his dinner..."

"Is taken care of. They shared a fried chicken dinner that I brought them from White Pines."

She regarded him suspiciously. "Something tells me that fried chicken was meant for you. Did you use it to bribe Dani to go along with this scheme of yours?"

He grinned. "What if I did? All it proves is that I will go to astonishing lengths to grab a few minutes alone with you."

"Don't," she commanded softly.

"Don't what?"

"Be nice to me."

"Why not?"

"I don't deserve it."

"Darlin', everyone deserves to have someone special be nice to them."

Tears spilled down her cheeks. "No, Justin. This can't be," she whispered, turning away.

She heard his quick movement, felt him behind her, but it was a long while before she felt his hand on her shoulder. It rested there gently, reminding her of his presence, soothing her but asking for nothing. The undemanding reassurance couldn't last forever, though. Sooner or later he would want something in return—answers, at the very least.

"Patsy?"

She sniffed and reached for a napkin to wipe away the dampness on her cheeks. Slowly he turned her to face him, then tucked a finger under her chin and lifted it until their gazes met.

"Tell me," he pleaded.

"I can't."

He brushed the hair back from her face, then lingered to caress her cheek. When he grazed her lower lip with the tip of his finger, the wonder of his gentleness almost shattered her. Slowly, so slowly that she told herself she must be mistaken, he lowered his head until their mouths were a scant hairsbreadth apart.

Hurry, hurry, she wanted to shout. If he rushed, if he simply stole the kiss, she could tell herself forever after that she hadn't wanted it to happen. But this way, there was no denying the pull, no pretending that she didn't want it with every fiber of her being. There was time enough for longing and more than enough time for guilt.

At the last possible second, when she could feel the warmth of his breath fanning over her flesh, honor intruded. She jerked away, moved until the width of the counter was safely between them again. She grasped the cool Formica merely to steady herself, but held so tightly that her knuckles turned white and the edge cut into her hand....

"I'm sorry," he said.

"No," she said adamantly. "You have nothing to be sorry for."

"I do," he insisted. "I knew better. I knew it wasn't what you wanted."

"But I did," she whispered, her voice thick with fresh, unshed tears. "More than anything."

"Why, then?"

Looking into his eyes, she saw that he already knew the answer, that he'd guessed it somehow.

"Who is he, Patsy?"

"Nobody," she said at once. "There's nobody."

Something that might have been pain flared in his eyes then. His expression turned weary. "You're lying," he said softly.

She turned away because she couldn't bear to see the hurt in his eyes.

"Maybe someday you'll realize you don't have to lie to me," he told her. "Maybe someday you'll trust me with the truth."

And maybe, she thought wistfully, maybe someday there would be angels to look out for women whose hearts had been every bit as battered as their psyches or their bodies.

Chapter Six

Justin cursed himself six ways from Sunday as he walked home after leaving Patsy at her front door. She'd barely said a word to him as she'd closed up Dolan's or as they'd walked up the block to Dani's.

At least he'd been wise enough not to pressure her any more by asking to come in or by walking on into his sister's clinic to say hi to Dani and Billy. No, for once he'd done the smart thing. He'd said good-night, reminded her of his promise to take Billy out for spaghetti the next night and left.

He figured it would be days and not hours before he forgot the wounded look in her eyes when he'd accused her of lying. Even though they both knew the accusation was true, pointing it out hadn't helped anything. Now she would only be more wary of him than ever. He regretted that almost as deeply as he regretted not getting to steal that kiss.

Of course, that had been a mistake, too. Had he forgotten so quickly Tate's warning to maintain his objectivity or, if he found he couldn't, to turn the unofficial investigation into Patsy's background over to Tate himself? He'd come damned close to blowing everything. For a man who prided himself on not crossing lines, he was virtually doing a hundred-yard dash across this one.

Distracted by his dark thoughts, he was halfway up the walk at home before he realized that someone was waiting in the shadows. Regretting that he didn't have his gun, he was preparing to launch himself at the intruder, when Harlan Patrick stepped into the light cast by the streetlight on the corner.

"Hey, Justin. You're late getting home."

"Damn you, do you know how close you came to getting tackled?" Justin muttered as he brushed past his cousin and unlocked his door. "You have a key. Why didn't you go inside to wait for me?"

"Because I just got here," he explained with exaggerated patience. "I saw you coming and waited out here. What the devil's wrong with you, anyway? Why are you so jumpy? This is Los Piños, not Dallas. How many criminals wait in shadows around here? For that matter, how many bad guys have you arrested lately, not counting those sickos who dared to let their parking meters run out?"

Harlan Patrick gave Justin a knowing look. "Wait. Forget I asked that. You let the last genuine lawbreaker go free, didn't you, and it's still stuck in your craw. This does have something to do with the mysterious stranger, doesn't it?"

"It's none of your business." Justin pushed past him and went into the kitchen, where he grabbed a soda from the almost barren refrigerator. "Want one?"

"Sure."

He tossed that can to his cousin, then grabbed another and popped the top. A long, cold drink did nothing to soothe his frayed temper.

"Justin?"

"Yeah."

"Is there a problem?"

"I wish to hell I knew for sure."

"What does that mean?"

"It means every instinct tells me there is, but I can't get a handle on it."

"Or do you just not like the answers you're coming up with?"

He sighed. "That, too," he admitted.

"Want to talk about it?"

"Not especially."

"I have tremendous insight into the female mind," Harlan Patrick claimed.

Justin hooted at that. "If playing the field counts for anything, I'm sure that's true. I'm just not so sure I want to take advice from a man who doesn't know the meaning of settling down."

"I am settling down. I haven't dated anyone but Laurie for months now."

"Really? Months? That must be some kind of record."

"I'd make it permanent if she'd hear of it, but she still has this crazy idea about going to Nashville as soon as she gets some money together."

"Maybe you ought to loan her the money," Justin suggested. "Let her get it out of her system."

"No way," Harlan Patrick said. "I'm not going to help set her up for heartache."

"She'll do it on her own, then. You know she will. And in the meantime, you'll be waiting around."

Harlan Patrick shook his head. "No way. She'll wake up one of these days and realize that it's only a foolish dream. Then we'll get married and raise a family out at White Pines. She'll switch from singing country to lullabies."

Justin had only spent a few evenings with Laurie Jensen, but even he could see that his cousin had a blind spot when it came to Laurie's commitment to her music. "If you believe that, then you don't know your lady half as well as you think you do," he warned. "Where is she tonight?"

"Over in Garden City, singing at a club."

"And what's she doing tomorrow?"

Harlan Patrick scowled. "Singing here in town."

"And you don't think that means anything?"

"Sure, it does. I don't object if she wants to sing every once in a while around here."

"That's mighty big of you. When was the last time Laurie asked your permission?"

Harlan Patrick's disgruntled expression was answer

enough. "Never mind," Justin said. "Wake up, cousin. The woman has the voice of an angel, a way with words and the ambition it takes to make her dream come true. Either help her or get out of her way."

"Who asked for your advice?"

"Consider it a gift from someone who's older and wiser."

"You can't be that wise, if you can't make heads or tails of what's going on with the town's newest resident. I thought cops had all sorts of ways to get answers if they wanted them badly enough."

That was the trouble, of course. Justin wasn't one bit sure he was ready to hear the answers, not from that computer down at the station, not even from Patsy's own lips.

Billy's cheeks were flushed, his straight black hair a damp fringe around his face. He smelled like talcum powder and baby.

"Which bedtime story tonight?" Patsy asked him, holding up the two books she'd taken from his shelves when they'd left home. There had been dozens more she'd left behind, but these two were Billy's favorites.

Bathing Billy had soothed her jangled nerves after that near kiss from Justin. That and the story were a familiar routine, one that had been repeated for so long, no matter where they were, that she could almost convince herself that their lives were normal.

Billy popped his thumb into his mouth and studied

the covers of the books as intently as if it were the first time he'd ever seen them. "Two stories," he pleaded finally.

"No, sweet pea. Only one."

A mutinous expression crossed his face. "Two."

"Choose or there will be no story at all." She moved to put the books away.

"No, Mama. Read rabbit story."

She grinned. Forced to choose, *The Velveteen Rabbit* was always the one he picked. "You must know it by heart."

"Don't care. Read it," he commanded with the same authoritative manner as his father.

"Please," she prompted.

"Please, Mama."

As she began reading the familiar words, Billy began to drift off. She was even more surprised, then, when he murmured, "Mama, where's Daddy?"

It was the first time he'd mentioned his father since they'd left home. She'd wondered more than once if that was because Will was so often away from home that Billy was used to not seeing him or if it was because he preferred this quiet, peaceful life without his father around.

"Daddy's at home in Oklahoma."

"Wanna see him."

Patsy sat back and tried to control the shaking that began deep inside. She hadn't wanted to believe that Billy would ever miss his daddy. She'd almost convinced herself that the disruption in their lives she'd brought on by running away hadn't fazed Billy at all.

After all, he and his father had spent precious little time together bonding. Obviously, though, what time they had shared had had a profound impact, one that weeks of separation hadn't dimmed.

Before she could think of anything at all to say, Billy crawled into her lap. "Please, Mama."

Patsy hugged him tightly. "Oh, baby, I know you miss your daddy, but it's not possible to see him right now."

"Please."

"Daddy's far away. He can't come visit."

"Wanna see him," Billy protested, tears welling up in his eyes.

Patsy rocked him. "Shh, baby. It's going to be okay," she promised.

How? a voice inside her head demanded. How was she going to make this right? She couldn't explain to a two-year-old that his daddy was a potential threat to both of them. For almost the first time since she'd left home, doubts began to crowd in.

Maybe she should call Will. Maybe by now he would have gotten the message that she wouldn't tolerate his behavior. Maybe he'd reform.

And maybe pigs would fly, she thought sarcastically. She knew better. How many women fell into that trap? How many convinced themselves that their husbands were truly sorry, that the psychological abuse or battering would never happen again? She wasn't going to delude herself that way. She wasn't going to wait for Will to actually slam his fist into her rather than an inanimate object.

Still she could take a drive one day, call Will from a public phone and let Billy talk to him. If she made the call far from Los Piños and kept it brief, surely he wouldn't be able ·to trace it, wouldn't be able to find them. Didn't she owe Billy that much at least?

She glanced down and saw that her son was finally asleep, his thumb tucked securely in his mouth. She shifted him into position on his bed, then pulled a sheet up over him. He'd kick it off in no time, but at least he could start the night covered up.

She stood for a long time, gazing down at him, then bent over and pressed a kiss to his flushed cheek. "I love you, angel. More than anything."

After she left him, she took her own bath, sinking into a sea of fragrant bubbles and trying to let her mind drift. Unfortunately, every time it did, an image of Justin Adams floated into view. Even the memory of his fingers against her cheek made her nipples hard. Recalling the exact instant when she'd known he was going to kiss her made her flesh heat. As the cooling bathwater lapped against her overheated flesh, she moaned softly.

Next time she might not be so strong. Next time she might accept the tenderness he was offering, the promise of even a few moments of gentle loving.

No. She brought herself back sharply from the provocative image. Stepping out of the tub, she toweled herself dry with rough strokes, then yanked on her robe. She didn't dare even begin to think that way about Justin. She was still married, if only in name. She was no doubt in a heap of trouble with Will, if not with the authorities. She couldn't drag Justin into the middle of all that.

Nor could she turn to a man to solve her problems. All her life, she had been relying on other people. First it had been her parents who'd set the rules and protected her from harm. She had left her hometown to prove that she could stand on her own two feet, only to fall in love with Will and let him take over the control of her life just as her parents had before him.

This time was going to be different. She was going to solve her own problems. She would settle this mess with Will, establish a solid, respectable future for herself and her son and then...well, then, if Justin was still interested, if the attraction hadn't died, maybe there could be something between them. Not if she needed his protection, though. Only if she could come to him as an equal, a woman every bit as strong and capable as he was.

"You're getting a little ahead of yourself," she chided herself aloud. "The man tried to kiss you. He didn't propose marriage."

But something told her that a man as honorable as Justin Adams had proved himself to be took even his kisses seriously and that she would be very wise to remember that.

Patsy barely had the door at Dolan's open in the morning when Justin came in. She switched on the lights and watched warily as he crossed to the counter and settled on a stool. If he brought up that almost kiss, she wasn't sure what she was going to say to him.

"I guess the coffee's not ready yet, is it?" he asked, his manner nothing more than friendly.

Patsy let out a sigh of relief. Apparently last night was forgotten. "I'm just about to put it on. It won't take a minute. Can I get you something else?"

"Take your time. I know it's not really opening time yet. I wanted to catch you alone."

Panic, never far away, choked her. "Why?" she asked, barely managing to get the single word out.

He seemed amused by the question. "To talk."

"About?"

"It can wait. Whenever you're set, I'll take eggs, bacon, toast."

She already knew he liked his eggs over easy, his bacon crisp and his toast the same color as his coffee—or so he claimed. She'd thought he was only being polite when she accidentally burned the first batch she ever made for him, but he swore burnt toast reminded him of home. She noticed, though, that he scraped away most of the black before eating it.

She was about to turn away to start his breakfast, when he snagged her hand.

"Patsy."

Her gaze met his, then skittered away. "Yes?"

"Maybe we should get this out of the way. I'm sorry about last night."

"There's nothing to be sorry for."

"I pushed."

"You've already apologized. It wasn't necessary then. It isn't now."

"But—"

"Justin, please," she pleaded. "Drop it."

His gaze locked with hers, questioning her even without any accompanying words. She held her breath, waiting for something, an explosion maybe. Will would have gone into a rage if she'd dared to cut him off.

Finally, to her relief, Justin simply nodded.

"For now."

It had become a refrain between them, a subtle warning that one day she would pay for all the silences. One day the questions would intensify and there would be no holding back. He would demand to know everything.

"I'll get your breakfast," she said, and hurried away.

By the time she'd fixed his eggs and bacon, Sharon Lynn had arrived and there were more customers. From then on Patsy was so busy she didn't have time to take a deep breath, much less worry about Justin and his unanswered questions.

If was well after nine before she got a real break.

"Sit for a minute," Sharon Lynn ordered. "I'll bring you a cup of coffee."

"You must be as beat as I am. Why should you wait on me?"

"Because you opened up this morning and Justin was right on your heels so I know perfectly well you haven't had a spare second since." She gave Patsy a curious look. "Everything okay between you and my cousin?"

"Of course," Patsy said a little too quickly. "Why wouldn't it be?"

"I just thought there might be some residual suspiciousness because of that incident when you first arrived. Justin's like a dog with a bone when things don't add up to him."

Patsy's hand stilled with the coffee halfway to her mouth. She regarded Sharon Lynn warily. "And you think things don't add up with me?"

"I didn't say that."

"But you believe Justin has doubts."

"He's a cop. Doubts are second nature to him. It doesn't mean I think he's right."

Fear streaked through her. What if Justin hadn't let things rest, after all? What if he'd dug up something? What if he knew all about her past and was waiting for her to open up and admit the trouble she was in? What if…?

"Has he said something?" she asked cautiously.

"No, but I've watched him around you. One second he looks like a man who's falling hard for a woman, the next he gets this wary expression in his eyes."

Patsy couldn't deny Sharon Lynn's perception. She'd seen the same reactions all too often herself.

"I'm sorry," Sharon Lynn said. "I shouldn't have said anything. I didn't mean to upset you. I don't want you to be on your guard every time he's around."

"I'm not upset. I can't blame Justin for the way he

feels. I was shoplifting when he first saw me. I offered to move on, to leave Los Piños. He assured me he could forget what happened, but maybe he can't. Maybe I should go.''

Sharon Lynn looked thunderstruck. ''No, absolutely not. Where would you go?''

''I don't know,'' Patsy admitted.

''Then put that idea right out of your head. Nobody wants you to leave.''

''Leave? Who's leaving?'' Justin demanded, walking up behind them.

Patsy turned slowly. ''I thought maybe it would be for the best if I did.''

''Well, it wouldn't,'' he said succinctly.

His sharp response hung in the air. For the longest time no one said anything.

''I'll be in the back if anyone needs me,'' Sharon Lynn said finally, but neither Justin nor Patsy spared her a glance.

''Are you sure you don't want me to go?'' she asked, searching his face.

''Yes, I'm sure. I just wish…'' His voice trailed off.

''Wish what?''

''That you felt you could be honest with me.''

Patsy wished that, too, more than she could say. She knew, too, that he could get most of the answers he craved just by running her license tag number. Obviously he hadn't, or he'd want to know why she'd lied about her name being Gresham, not Longhorn.

Either he was waiting for her to come to him with the truth on her own or he was afraid of it.

"I can't," she said simply. "I wish I could, but I can't."

"Will you tell me one thing?"

"If I can."

"Have you broken any laws?"

"No," she said honestly. Not unless Will had manufactured a crime out of her leaving with their son.

Relief washed some of the tension out of his expression. "Then we'll leave it at that."

She grinned. "For now."

He chuckled at her repetition of his favorite warning. "Who knows? Maybe I'll just drop it for good. Maybe I'll just take it on faith that you'll tell me the whole story when you feel you can."

Patsy regarded him skeptically. "Can you do that?"

He started to answer, then sighed. "Probably not," he admitted regretfully.

"That's what makes you a good cop, Deputy."

"Maybe it doesn't make me such a terrific man. I ought to trust you. I want to."

"I've given you plenty of cause not to."

He lifted his hand, hesitated, then, looking as if he wanted to do so much more, he gently grazed her cheek with his knuckles. "You know what I wish more than anything?"

Dazed by the look of pure longing in his eyes, Patsy shook her head.

"I wish that I knew whether I had any right at all to kiss you."

She shuddered with a longing that was equal to his, then finally looked away.

Justin sighed. "That pretty much answers my question, doesn't it?"

With her eyes squeezed tightly shut to keep the tears from falling, she said softly, "Yes, I suppose it does."

It was only a tiny hint at the whole truth, but it was enough to put a bleak expression on Justin's face and send him striding out of Dolan's without a backward glance.

It was also more than enough to break Patsy's heart in two.

Chapter Seven

With Justin gone, Patsy was left all alone to battle tears and guilt and shame. How could she go on deceiving a man who had been nothing but kind to her, a man who'd already put aside his own convictions about right and wrong to give her a break? She was still wrestling with that when Sharon Lynn came out of the back.

Patsy hastily wiped her eyes and forced a smile. She didn't want this compassionate woman to be caught in the middle. It was too soon to test the strength of their friendship, especially when Justin was part of her family. She knew enough about the Adamses by now to know that they were bound tight by love and loyalty.

"Everything okay?" Sharon Lynn asked, concern etched on her face.

"Fine."

"You don't look fine. You look as if you've been crying." Her expression turned indignant. "If that cousin of mine has done anything to upset you, I'll tear him limb from limb."

The fierce promise startled Patsy, then left her chuckling. "Don't you think it would be a bit of a mismatch?" she asked.

"Hey, I grew up playing with him and my brother. I'm as tough as they are. I had to be." Sharon Lynn winked. "I'm also a better shot."

Patsy shuddered at the teasing suggestion. "Please, you don't need to prove it on my account. I don't think there will be any need to resort to guns. Justin didn't deliberately upset me. I'm the one responsible for him taking off in such a foul humor. It was all my fault."

She deliberately pushed her own concerns over Justin aside. Now seemed like a really good time to change the subject and focus on that night's surprise bridal shower before Sharon Lynn wanted to know exactly what she'd done that was so terrible.

"Don't forget we're having dinner tonight," she reminded Sharon Lynn.

For a moment Sharon Lynn seemed startled by the abrupt shift in topic. "Patsy, don't you want to talk about what just happened here?"

"No," she said honestly. "I'd rather think about the pleasant evening we're going to have. It's been a long time since I've invited company over. You haven't forgotten, have you?"

"No, of course not, but there's no reason you should cook after standing in front of the grill here all day. Why don't we go out?" she suggested. "We can let somebody else cook for both of us for a change."

Patsy thought of all the people who'd be waiting in her living room and almost panicked. "Absolutely not," she said hurriedly and began improvising. "I already have everything ready. It won't take a minute to get dinner on the table."

"But you must not get a chance to go out with friends very often because of Billy. Since he'll be with Justin, it would be the perfect time to get out and kick up your heels a little."

"Believe me, the last thing I want to do is kick up my heels," she said with heartfelt sincerity.

Patsy studied her intently, then nodded. "If you're sure…"

"I am."

The rest of the afternoon was so busy the only words they had time to exchange were about orders. By the time they closed up, both of them were dead on their feet. Even so, Patsy couldn't help feeling excited as she and Sharon Lynn headed for her place and the waiting bridal shower. She was grateful she'd been asked to play even a minor role in the surprise. It made her feel as if she belonged, as if she had a contribution to make, something she hadn't felt in a very long time.

When they reached the house, she was taken aback by its deserted look. Not even Dani's car was in the driveway, and there were no extra cars parked along the block. Where was everyone? Had she gotten it wrong, after all? If she had, the big surprise for Sharon Lynn was going to be the fact that there was no dinner waiting in the fridge.

Taking it on faith that there was a surprise party waiting inside, she unlocked the door, then led the way into the living room. It wasn't dark yet, but the room was filled with shadows. Just as she was about to reach for a light switch, someone else turned on the overhead light and the room erupted with noise. People burst in from the clinic, where they'd obviously been hiding. All the shouts of "Surprise!" set off the animals. The dogs began howling and the cats scurried for cover.

In the midst of the chaos, Sharon Lynn stared around at all of her friends and family, then burst into tears.

"Oh, dear," Patsy murmured, stunned by the reaction. She put an arm around her. "What's wrong? Please, don't cry."

Sharon Lynn waved off the sympathy. "I'm okay. It's just…"

"It's just that she's never gotten this far before," Jenny said, coming over to envelop her in a hug. "It's only a little over a week and counting to the big day."

Sharon Lynn mopped at her eyes. "I'm actually beginning to believe it's going to happen this time." She turned to Patsy and said with mock severity, "As for you, you are a very sneaky lady. I had no idea what you were up to. No wonder you turned down my offer to go out for dinner.''

''Thank goodness you didn't insist on it. I'm not sure what I would have come up with to get you over here. As for the rest, I didn't really do anything,'' Patsy said. ''Jenny and Dani did all the planning and the work. I was just brought in at the last second to deliver you. I still think I ought to get Billy and go out to eat, while you all celebrate.''

''Absolutely not,'' Dani said, joining them. ''Besides, Justin already has Billy. The boy has my brother wound around his little finger. I believe they were going to stop at the toy store on the way to dinner. Justin saw a remote control police car in there he wanted to check out.''

''Oh, dear,'' Patsy murmured. ''Maybe I should—''

''You should relax and enjoy yourself,'' Jenny told her. ''Let Justin spend a little of his money for a change. It'll do him good to hang out in a toy store. Maybe he'll rediscover the kid inside. He's not even thirty and already he's turned into a straitlaced old man.''

''You've got that right,'' Sharon Lynn said. ''When I think of how much mischief he and Harlan used to get into, it's hard to believe it's the ___.''

''___ ladies,'' an older woman with the same ___ny said. ''I'm starving and you know ___ will start worrying if I'm out too ___ u know he'll use it as an excuse to come looking for me. As it is, he's very put out that he wasn't invited to the shower. Just give him the slightest excuse and he'll race into town.''

"Maybe it would be worth it," Dani said with a wicked twinkle in her eyes. "I can just see Grandpa Harlan's expression when Sharon Lynn starts opening packages filled with slinky lingerie.''

"If Mom's half the woman I know she is, it won't be anything he hasn't seen before," Jenny teased, bringing a blush to the older woman's cheeks.

"Patsy, have you met Janet yet?" Dani asked. "She's married to Grandpa Harlan and she claims to give him a run for his money, but as you just heard, the man has the original feminist in the family on a short leash.''

Janet winked. "I just let him think that. Now that I've closed my law practice, I do my level best to drive him crazy. It's the only thing I have to look forward to.''

Patsy regarded her intently. "You're a lawyer?''

"One of the best in the business," Jenny said proudly. "She was also a real activist for Native American rights. If you ever have a legal problem, you couldn't find anyone in town to give you b advice.''

Patsy tucked that piece of information away other time. Could this woman with the wis kind eyes be the answer to her prayers? a lot about Native American affairs, w know if Patsy's position would be w tody battle because she wasn't Nati fear that tribal law would come into play had been nagging at her from the moment she decided to run. She had been terrified that that was the unspoken threat Will would use to take her baby away.

"Hey, why so solemn?" Jenny asked, studying her worriedly.

Patsy forced a smile. "Sorry. Don't let my mood spoil the party."

"She and Justin had a little set-to earlier," Sharon Lynn explained.

"Oh, really?" Janet said, her expression thoughtful. "I haven't seen Justin riled up much. He's always been a pretty even-tempered guy."

"Put him in a room with Patsy for ten minutes and watch the fireworks," Sharon Lynn suggested.

"Interesting," Janet said.

"Okay, enough of this. Forget Justin. He's just a man. Nothing is going to ruin this shower," Jenny said adamantly. "It's been too long coming, right, Sharon Lynn?"

"Way too long," Sharon Lynn replied fervently. She beckoned to Patsy. "Come with me. I hear there's a huge Tex-Mex buffet in the dining room and the word is that the housekeeper at White Pines made the food. Maritza's enchiladas are to die for."

From that moment on, everyone made a deliberate effort to include Patsy in the celebration. By the time it was over, she had pushed aside the words she had exchanged with Justin and her worries over a custody battle for Billy. For a couple of hours, she actually managed to live in the moment. More than being accepted as a stranger in their midst, she felt as if she were part of this large extended family.

If only it were true, she thought wistfully as the last of them left. Surrounded by their strength, she was pretty sure she could face just about anything.

As she helped Sharon Lynn pile the last of the packages into the back of her car, Justin came up the walk, carrying a sleeping Billy in his arms. He grinned at Sharon Lynn.

"Looks like you picked up a lot of loot. Any sexy lingerie in there?"

"None that you'll ever see," Sharon Lynn told him. "You find your own woman and your own sexy lingerie."

Justin's gaze shifted instantly to Patsy. She could feel her cheeks burning as he studied her thoughtfully. To cover her rush of embarrassment, she reached for her son.

"I'll take Billy."

"No need," Justin countered, his expression turning stubborn. "I'll carry him in to bed." He held out a huge sack. "You can take this, though."

She reached for the bag and almost dropped it. "What on earth?"

"Billy and I did a little shopping."

Remembering what Jenny had said earlier, she asked, "For yourself or for him?"

He grinned. "He's promised to let me come over and play with his new toys every now and then."

"Justin, you really shouldn't have."

"Of course I should. I haven't had so much fun in

years. Wait till you see this really nifty police car. It even has a siren.''

Sharon Lynn regarded him with amusement. "I thought you had your own police car with a siren.''

The comment didn't seem to faze him. "Yeah, but Billy didn't,'' he said matter-of-factly.

As far as Patsy knew, Billy had never expressed any interest in having a remote control car. As Jenny had suggested earlier, she suspected the toy really was for Justin, bought under the guise of a gift. She hefted the bag, which weighed a ton.

"There's more than a car in here, isn't there?''

"We saw a basketball set that was pretty snazzy, too.''

Patsy stared. "Basketball? Billy's two. It'll be a long time before he can even hold a basketball, much less play hoops with someone your size.''

"This is a toddler basketball set. The net's only as high as my waist and the ball weighs about five ounces. It's not exactly regulation.''

"I see. Anything else?''

"A surprise for you. Billy picked it out.''

"At the toy store?''

"Yep.''

Sharon Lynn regarded them both with tolerant amusement. "Looks like it's your turn for surprises, Patsy. I'll just run along now and leave you to it.''

"Don't go," she said in a rush. She didn't want to be left alone with this man whose every action charmed her and reminded her of how long it had been since anyone at all had given a thought to what might make her happy.

"I have a long drive," Sharon Lynn said, ignoring the plea and getting into her car. "See you two in the morning." She blew a kiss in Patsy's direction. "Thanks again for everything."

After she'd gone, Patsy seemed to be rooted to the spot. It was Justin who finally said, "I think maybe I ought to get Billy into bed before he wakes up."

Flustered, she murmured, "Yes, of course."

Inside, she followed him into Billy's room. She took off Billy's shoes and socks, then stripped off his shorts. She left his spaghetti-stained T-shirt on, fearful that removing it would awaken him. He settled onto his tummy, his thumb going instinctively into his mouth.

She glanced up and caught an odd expression on Justin's face, something that might have been long-ing.

"He's a terrific kid," he said softly.

"He's the light of my life," she said. "I don't know what I'd ever do if something happened to him."

Justin's gaze shifted to her. "What could happen?"

Realizing that she'd almost given her very real fears away, she said, "You know, any of the million and one things that can happen to a kid."

Justin shook his head. "You sounded as if you had something very specific in mind," he said, seizing on her slip of the tongue.

"No," she protested. "Just the usual worries any parent has."

His piercing gaze was unrelenting. "Why don't I believe you?"

"Because not believing me has become second nature to you."

He continued to study her intently, then finally sighed and relaxed. "Okay, maybe my cop's instincts have been on overdrive since we met. I'll try to let up."

Patsy recognized it for the futile promise it was. Rather than debating it with him again, she poked at the bag she'd dropped on the floor. "Okay, where's my surprise?"

Justin picked up the sack and carried it into the living room. "Close your eyes."

She did as she was told and waited with as much anticipation as she might have the promise of a kiss. Her heart skipped a beat. Her pulse pounded.

"Hold out your hands."

She held them out in front of her. A second later she felt something soft and fluffy being placed in her hands. She opened her eyes and saw a toy dog that looked so real she was certain it would begin to bark at any second. The terrier look-alike was caramel colored and had a pink tongue so real looking she expected him to lick her fingers.

"He's wonderful," she said, hugging him to her.

"Billy said you liked dogs. I figured I shouldn't try getting you a real one without discussing it with you, but this looked like the next best thing."

"He feels real," she said, running her fingers through the curling plush hair. "And look at these eyes. He's staring right at me."

"Have you ever had a dog?"

She shook her head. "My parents both worked. They didn't think it was right to leave a dog home alone all day." And Will hadn't wanted anything that might mess up the house and spoil his image if a reporter happened to drop by unexpectedly.

"You could have one now," Justin suggested.

She gestured toward the cats that were curled hither and yon in the living room. "What about them?"

"They're used to every kind of animal under the sun. Dani's a vet, remember? She's spent her whole life taking in every stray that wandered by. She might have one next door even as we speak."

"Several," she conceded, thinking of the cacophony of sound they'd set off earlier. She grinned. "There's always Punk."

"That's not a dog. That's a beast."

"He has his own home, anyway. His owners are due back any day now."

"You sound sad about it."

"I've gotten used to him. Punk and I have an understanding. I sneak him treats and he doesn't lick me to death."

Justin grinned. "See what I mean? You're a natural pet owner. Think about it," he encouraged.

Getting a dog of her own would make a statement of sorts, she realized, if only to herself. It would mean that she intended to stay right here, that she was beginning to put down roots. It would also finalize her decision never to return to Will.

"I'll think about it," she said, then stroked the toy dog in her lap. "In the meantime, Chester here will do just fine."

"Chester?"

She shrugged. "I have no idea why. The name just came to me."

He grinned. "Don't expect me to argue with divine inspiration." He stood and headed for the door, then paused. "I'm glad you like the surprise."

"I *love* the surprise," she said emphatically. It was the very best one she could remember.

With Sharon Lynn's wedding only a few days away, the burden for running Dolan's fell on Patsy's shoulders. She was grateful for the responsibility. It kept her so busy she didn't have time to think about how much longer she could continue with this charade before Justin found out the rest of the truth.

"You're sure you can handle things if I'm gone today?" Sharon Lynn asked for the umpteenth time.

"I can handle it," Patsy repeated, also for the umpteenth time.

"You remember how Mrs. Jenkins likes her eggs?"

"Scrambled moist," Patsy dutifully recited.

"And Tate prefers—"

"Rye toast, not plain."

"What about Doc Dolan?"

"He likes egg salad on white for lunch with a scoop of potato salad on the plate."

Sharon Lynn nodded. "Yes, perfect." She started for the door, then turned back. "I won't be back from Dallas before seven. I've got the fitting for the wedding dress, then a meeting with the florist and a late lunch with two of my bridesmaids, women I went to high school with who're living in Dallas now."

"I can close up," Patsy reassured her. "I'll leave the day's deposit in the night drop at the bank. You've shown me what to do."

"I know. I just hate dumping all this on you."

"You're not dumping anything on me. You told me, when you hired me, you were getting married and that I'd have extra work. Stop worrying and get going before you miss your final fitting."

"Given the number of times Kyle and I almost made it to the altar in the past, you'd think I'd have this down to a science by now."

"Well, this time's the charm. It's less than a week till the wedding and everything's going smoothly, right?"

"I suppose."

Patsy studied her intently. "Sharon Lynn, is there something else worrying you?"

"Not really. I suppose it's just panic. There's been one crisis or another every time the wedding date got close. I'm afraid we're jinxed."

"I don't believe in jinxes. Now go, before your uncle Jordan pitches a fit. He is flying you over, isn't he?"

"Yes, and you're right. He's always in a rush. I'll call you later just to see if anything's come up."

"If you call, I'll be insulted."

Sharon Lynn grinned. "Okay, okay." She paused to hug Patsy. "Thank you. You've been a godsend."

"So have you," Patsy replied quietly. "More than you know."

Sharon Lynn gave her an odd little look, but she let whatever questions she had die on her lips. Finally she smiled and said again, "Thanks."

"Go."

"Let me check—"

"Sharon Lynn!"

"Okay, I'm out of here."

Justin met her in the doorway. "It's a good thing," he said. "I just got a call from Dad. He's at the airport and he's getting really irritated. You were supposed to be there a half hour ago. He has a business meeting he's going to miss if you don't hit the road right this second."

"Why didn't he call me?"

"Because apparently your phone is dead or off the hook."

"Oh, my God," she murmured as the color drained from her face. She raced into the back room.

Patsy and Justin exchanged an amused look, then followed. They caught Sharon Lynn putting the receiver back into place.

"I laid it down to look for my wedding checklist while I was talking to Mom," she explained sheepishly. "I guess I got distracted."

Justin shook his head. "Which explains why I had a call from your mother, as well," he said with tolerant amusement. "Maybe I'd better drive you to the airport."

Sharon Lynn looked oddly relieved. "Would you? You're a doll."

Justin turned and winked at Patsy. "Remember that, would you?"

"No need," she said. "I already knew it."

He seemed startled by her reply. He hesitated as if there were something more on his mind, but Sharon Lynn clutched his arm and dragged him away.

"I'll be back," he promised. "And I won't forget what you said."

Patsy's heart skipped a beat. He was making far too big a thing out of a casual admission, she thought. Had she known he would? Was that why she'd said it?

Of course not, she consoled herself. It had just been a teasing response to his own deliberate taunt. It had been so long since she'd engaged in even the most innocent flirting, she'd forgotten that it could be taken seriously. She hadn't meant to light that fire in his eyes. Surely she hadn't meant to undo all she'd done to keep him at a distance. Justin had simply read too much into it.

The fact remained that he was going to be back here in no time and he was going to have expectations of one sort or another. And she was going to have to think of yet another lie to push him away, when all she really wanted was for him to sweep her into his arms and never let go.

Was that why she'd tempted fate just now? Had she wanted him to take the decision out of her hands at last? Had she deliberately prompted him into making a move so that she wouldn't have to hold herself accountable? Was that the kind of woman she'd become?

She was still debating with herself and not liking any of the answers she came up with, when a man with white hair and the impish grin of every Adams she'd ever run across walked in and sauntered up to the counter. He settled on a stool, then looked her over with blatant fascination.

"Can I help you?" she said, trying not to flinch under that penetrating scrutiny.

"That depends. Are you Patsy Gresham?"

She nodded.

"I'm Harlan Adams. Since no one's seen fit to bring you by the ranch to meet me, I figured it was up to me to perform the introductions. I'm Justin's granddaddy."

"Yes, sir."

His gaze never wavered. "And you're the woman who's managed to tie that boy into knots." Another grin broke across his face. "Congratulations!"

Patsy swallowed hard. "Sir, I don't know what you've heard, but I think you've got it all wrong. Justin and I are just friends. Acquaintances, really."

"Girl, I don't care what you call it, as long as you bring some joy into his life."

She was stunned by his analysis. "Actually, all I've brought into his life so far is aggravation," she said, to set the record straight.

He chuckled at that. "So much the better. Now I want you to come to White Pines for dinner tomorrow night. Bring that little one of yours, too. The place will be crawling with my grandbabies. One more won't make a bit of difference. In fact, the whole family will be there."

"Then won't I be out of place?"

"I invited you, didn't I? Besides, it's a little get-together in Sharon Lynn's honor. You belong there."

"Yes, but—"

He got off the stool and headed for the door. "Seven o'clock sharp. Maritza gets downright testy if her food gets cold."

He was gone before Patsy could argue. One thing his visit had proved, though. The Adams men were bossy as the very dickens and she was pretty sure most of them always got their own way. It was one more thing she needed to keep in mind when she was dealing with Justin.

Chapter Eight

Justin's day went from bad to worse. After he dropped Sharon Lynn off at the small local airport, he got a call about a prowler at the home of an elderly woman. More than likely it was her overly vivid imagination, but he couldn't ignore the call. Once Letty Jane got to talking, though, it took an act of God to get him away from the place. Literally.

A late morning thunderstorm rolled in with unexpected force, toppling a line of trees. Everyone vowed it hadn't been a twister, but Justin couldn't prove that by the damage the wind had done. It had upended a trailer on an acre of isolated property on the opposite side of town from Letty Jane's. He spent all day running to and fro, from one crisis to the next, never settling in one place long enough even to call Patsy and explain why he hadn't gotten back.

Not that she was likely to mind, he conceded. He'd seen the quick flaring of panic in her eyes when he'd promised to return. He'd known he was pushing again, but he hadn't been able to help it. There was something between them and he intended to do whatever it took to force her to admit she felt it, too.

After that, they could worry together about the consequences, assuming there was anything that needed worrying about.

Which he still didn't know, he reminded himself with a weary sigh.

As he drove back into town he told himself it was only natural to be going down Main Street just to see that all was right with his little world, even though a shortcut would have gotten him home more quickly. It didn't have anything at all to do with hoping to catch a glimpse of Patsy, either at Dolan's or at her own place.

Unfortunately, the drugstore was locked up tight, the only light the red glow of the exit sign inside the door. Patsy's was just as dark. He tried to tell himself it was just as well. He was exhausted and filthy. Even if she'd opened her arms and invited him in, he was too damned tired to do much about it. He satisfied himself with just knowing that she was all tucked in for the night.

He drove on to the sheriff's office. He could get a cup of coffee there, do his paperwork and head on home for a shower and a good night's sleep. Tomorrow would be soon enough to pursue things with Patsy. Tomorrow or the next day.

Or the day after that, if she had her way.

"My, my, you're a pretty sight," Tate Owens observed when Justin dragged into the station.

"Fortunately, you're not paying me according to my appearance," he retorted. "This is what happens when you slog around in a foot of mud for a few hours chasing down a woman's belongings."

"It surely was a mess out there," Tate agreed.

"I noticed you didn't linger long enough to muss the crease in your trousers," Justin commented good-naturedly. They both knew that Tate wasn't above getting filthy if there was a need for it. Today Justin had had things under control without his help.

Despite the jest, Tate's expression turned serious. "Becky called. Something came in over the wire she thought I ought to see."

A solemn note in Tate's voice alerted Justin that it was something he needed to see as well. "About Patsy Gresham?"

The sheriff nodded and handed over a flyer. "Her name's Longhorn," he said. "And she's got a husband over in Oklahoma who's been looking for her for a while now. Seems like she's been gone since just a little before she showed up here."

Justin stared blankly at the missing persons flyer. The picture was a family portrait—Patsy, Billy and a man who had to be her husband, Will Longhorn, according to the information at the bottom. For some reason that picture reminded him of a damned campaign poster. Even though the three of them were at some sort of outdoor picnic, there was a posed quality to it, a perfection to the lighting that suggested it had been taken by a professional, rather than some family member or a cooperative stranger.

"They look happy enough, don't they?" Tate said, his tone gentle.

Justin told himself it was his boss's tone, the hint of pity, that made him want to start throwing things. It had nothing to do with the gut-sick feeling in the pit of his stomach at the sight of Patsy with another man.

"You going to talk to her about this or am I?" Tate asked.

Justin stared at him in surprise. "You haven't reported her to the Oklahoma authorities yet?"

"Hell, no," Tate declared. "I figure she's a grown-up woman. If she's here, instead of there, there must be a reason for it. I'm not turning her over to them until I know a hell of a lot more than I do right now. You see anything on there about a crime? No. She's just a missing person. And while I think her family probably has a right to know she's safe, I don't think it's my place to go about giving her away until I hear her side of it." His gaze was steady. "Or until you do."

"I'll talk to her," Justin said, his heart aching. The poster in his hands was proof that Patsy Gresham— Patsy Longhorn—was more out of his reach than ever. "How much time do I have?"

"I can bury that poster on my desk. Given the amount of paperwork piled up, it could take me a mighty long time to find it again. On the other hand, my conscience says a week at the outside.''

Justin nodded. It was more than he'd hoped for. ''I'll get the answers we need,'' he said grimly. ''You can count on it.''

Patsy had never met anyone like the Adams clan. They stuck together. And while there seemed to be a whole crowd of them, there was always room for a stranger in their midst.

The dinner she'd been invited to at White Pines had been a revelation. Harlan Adams's ranch was bigger by far than the ostentatious house Will had insisted they buy, yet White Pines was a home. There was no mistaking the warmth and love in every single room.

To her amazement, though, there had been no sign of Justin by dinnertime. No one had made excuses for him, either. When he'd appeared just in time for dessert, everyone had accepted his arrival without question.

If he'd been surprised to see her, he hadn't shown it. But he'd also seemed to be avoiding her the past few days, making her wonder if he was angry about her inclusion in the family event. Maybe she'd misread his intentions toward her, or maybe they'd just changed.

It was obvious he'd been startled again today when she'd walked into the wedding reception for Sharon Lynn. She hadn't made it to the church, because she'd filled in at Dolan's in the morning so everyone else could go to the service. But Sharon Lynn and Doc Dolan had insisted she close up and come to the reception. Neither of them had taken no for an answer.

"I intend to toss my bouquet straight at you, so you'd better be prepared," Sharon Lynn had told her.

The teasing remark had brought tears and a fresh bout of guilt she hadn't been able to explain.

The dance music was just starting when she walked into the huge tent that had been set up on the lawn at the ranch. Justin had been laughing with his cousins, but the laughter had died when he'd spotted her. This time, though, it seemed he didn't intend to avoid her. He made his way across the room and ended up at her side.

"What a wonderful party," she said, forcing a smile to go along with the lighthearted small talk. "Sharon Lynn looks radiant. And Kyle looks dazed."

"I don't think he can believe it's finally happened. It took them a long time to make this trip down the aisle. They deserve to be happy." His gaze locked with hers. "Everyone does."

She sensed at once that there was a deeper meaning behind his words, but for the life of her she couldn't imagine what it was. There was a vague hint of the old suspicion, the old caution, back in his expression, too.

Rather than ignoring the undercurrents as she once would have done, she addressed them directly. "Justin, are you upset that I came?"

He looked vaguely guilty at the pointed question. "No, of course not."

"Are you sure? I know there's nothing between us."

"Not for lack of trying on my part," he said.

She persisted, determined to apologize for intruding where she didn't belong. "I'm sorry if finding me at all these family functions the past few days is making you uncomfortable. Your grandfather and Sharon Lynn, they insisted I come."

"I'm sure," he said ruefully. He shook his head. "No, I'm the one who should be apologizing. We're a family of meddlers. With Sharon Lynn married off tonight, I'm the next logical target. Next week or next month it'll be Harlan Patrick's turn. I'm sorry you got caught in the cross fire."

"I don't mind," she confessed with a catch in her voice, uncertain what sort of reaction the admission might draw.

He regarded her with surprise. "Really? Now that is a change."

"It's true."

In fact, if the truth were known, she liked being linked to this strong, decent man whose temper never seemed to get the better of him. She'd seen his patience tested to the limits—by her, in fact—but he'd never once raised his voice. It was a welcome relief after Will.

If things were different, if she were free, a man like Justin Adams would be the kind of man she'd like in her life.

If she were free...

But she wasn't, and because she wasn't, she turned

and hurried away, ignoring Justin's commands for her to stop. She didn't slow until she was locked in a bathroom upstairs, far from the crowd of well-wishers.

She should leave, not just White Pines, but Los Piños. There was something different about Justin tonight, something that warned her away, told her that she'd stayed too long, tempting fate.

But if she took even a second to look into her heart, she knew that no matter the consequences, she couldn't go. The time for running was over.

"Getting any ideas, son?" Grandpa Harlan asked Justin as Sharon Lynn and Kyle moved into each other's arms for the first dance at the reception.

The question's timing couldn't have been worse, because he was getting ideas, had had them for a long time now, but he now knew for a fact they would never be. That poster on Tate's desk was evidence of that. Patsy belonged to another man. He'd guessed it weeks ago, but the proof had torn him apart.

"Don't you start, old man," he said, trying to take the sting out of his words.

His grandfather was made of hearty stuff. The order didn't faze him.

"I've seen the way you look at that pretty little gal from Oklahoma," he said, casting a sly look across the room to where Patsy was standing all alone. "You've got a thing for her. Why not admit it?"

Justin sighed. "Because there are things you don't

know, Grandpa Harlan, things I'm not even sure about. Seems like we just weren't meant to be.''

''Such as?''

Justin hesitated, then decided that his grandfather might be the one person on earth who could give him the kind of levelheaded advice he desperately needed right now. ''I think she's on the run.''

His grandfather took that news in stride. ''From the law?'' he demanded indignantly. ''I don't believe it. If that girl's some sort of criminal, then I'm no judge of character.''

''Maybe not from the law,'' Justin conceded. ''More likely from a man, possibly her husband.''

That did raise his grandfather's eyebrows ever so slightly. ''She's married? You know that for a fact?''

There was the missing persons report, but that was only one side of the story, just as Tate had suggested. ''Not exactly,'' he said eventually.

''Well, if you suspect it's the case, why the dickens haven't you asked her? From what I've seen, both of you have a lot riding on the truth.''

''I'm not sure she'd tell me the truth,'' Justin admitted. ''I see how skittish she is around me whenever I'm wearing my uniform. Tate flat out terrifies her. If she's going to open up, it might not be to one of us.''

What if she knew about the poster, guessed they'd seen it? he wondered. Would she run again? Was she that desperate to get away from her husband? He sighed. He couldn't get into that with his grandfather. He'd probably told him more than he should as it was.

"I keep hoping she'll explain on her own and let me help."

His grandfather regarded him with sympathy. "I think I see the position you're in. There's your duty as a sworn lawman. And, then, there's your duty to a woman you care about."

"Which one's more important?" Justin asked, aware that the question sounded a little plaintive. "I always thought for sure I knew. The law's the law."

"It's a delicate balancing act, all right," his grandfather said. "Maybe there's a way for both to be the same."

"How?"

"You won't know until you know all the truth. Talk to her, son. Do it now, tonight, before your courage fails you and before the answers can cut too deep."

"Too late for that," Justin said. "I'm already in way over my head."

"Then you'll find a way to make things right," his grandfather said with absolute confidence. "For both of you."

"I hope you're right."

"Well, of course I am," his grandfather said with exaggerated indignation. "You don't get to be my age without learning a thing or two. Now, go along. Talk to her. Unless I miss my guess, she's as torn up inside as you are."

Justin knew his grandfather was right. There was no way around it. This was one time he couldn't afford to be endlessly patient. Lives and futures were at stake. Patsy's and Billy's, maybe. His own for sure.

He weaved through the crowd, his gaze locked on the woman who stood all alone on the fringes. She looked more fragile than ever in a pale blue slip dress that skimmed over her body in a silken caress. The dress was the epitome of costly simplicity. It practically had designer stamped all over it. The cop in him had wanted to check for a label and demand explanations once again for the inconsistencies in her lifestyle. The man simply wanted to slide it over her head and run callused hands over the woman beneath.

If he listened to the throbbing in his veins, that dress would be merely an inconvenience. If he listened to his head, he would escort her somewhere very public for the conversation that had been too long coming. By the time he reached her side, he still wasn't sure which side had won the mental debate.

"Everything okay?" he asked, his tone cautious.

"Of course," she said, a little too brightly.

"Where'd you run off to?"

"The ladies' room."

"I thought maybe you were running away?"

Alarm flared in her eyes, but she quickly hid it. "From what?"

"Me."

"You don't scare me."

"I should."

"Why?"

"Because I want you."

She swallowed hard at the bold assertion. "I know."

"Any objections?"

Her hesitation—combined with the pure desire written all over her face—was enough to tell him as much as he needed to know. She wanted him all right, but she was going to do the honorable thing—the *wifely* thing—and say yes. She was going to tell him to take a hike.

Before she could say anything, he said quietly, "Let's go somewhere for coffee."

She blinked in surprise. "Coffee?"

"Don't argue. You don't want the alternative."

Her gaze locked with his. "I didn't say that."

His smile was forced. "You didn't have to. Come on, darlin', before I change my mind. Sharon Lynn and Kyle will be leaving any minute now, anyway."

Before she could object, he clasped her hand and dragged her along behind him, nodding politely to everyone they passed. It was a neat trick to get away from White Pines without being subjected to a million and one questions, but he managed it.

As he headed for his car, Patsy began to voice her first objection. "My car—"

He refused to relinquish his grip on her. "I'll have someone drive it into town in the morning."

Only after they were in his car with the radio playing at top volume to drown out any need for conversation did she speak again. Raising her voice to be heard, she asked, "Justin, what's going on?"

"We'll talk when we get into town."

"What's wrong with here?"

"I can't concentrate on you and the road at the same time."

He thought he caught the beginnings of a smile at that.

"Ever heard of small talk?"

"That's the last thing I want to engage in with you." To make his point, he reached for the volume and turned it up another notch. Now there was nothing in the car but the sound of George Strait and a sizzling tension for which there would be no relief.

In town, he parked in front of the Italian restaurant, knowing that it would be virtually empty at this hour, especially with half the folks in town out at White Pines at the wedding reception. The coffee was strong enough to keep them both wide-awake until they'd hashed this mess through from beginning to end.

He led the way to a booth with Patsy trailing along behind, silently fuming. He could practically feel the anger radiating from her. He couldn't say he blamed her, but he wasn't exactly dancing with joy tonight himself.

"Two coffees," he told the waitress in a tone that warned her not to linger.

"Sure, Justin." She left without asking about the wedding, returned with two cups and a whole pot of coffee, then retreated all the way into the kitchen.

"Look," Patsy began, scowling at him, "I don't know what has you in such a snit tonight, but you don't have any business taking it out on her, or on me, for that matter."

Justin sighed. "You're right."

"Then what's this all about?"

He looked into her eyes and saw the beginnings of wariness again. "Same old thing," he said, trying to make light of it.

"You think I'm hiding something."

"I *know* you're hiding something," he corrected.

She began twisting the napkin she was holding into a tight knot. She looked everywhere in the restaurant except at him. When the napkin shredded, she stared at it in dismay.

"Patsy, please, can't you tell me the truth after all this time? Maybe I can help."

The tears welling up in her eyes were almost his undoing. He wanted to take back all the questions. He wanted to promise that he would never pry into her past again, but it was too late for that. If he didn't, Tate would. It was better if he did it, if the truth was something shared between them, instead of a barrier they could never overcome.

"You can't," she whispered finally. "You can't help."

"I can try."

She shook her head. "This isn't the kind of problem you can fix with a screwdriver or even a hankie," she said, accepting the one he offered with a rueful smile.

"Neither of us will really know that until you tell me." He looked directly into her eyes then, willing her to begin at the beginning and tell him everything.

She opened her mouth, about to speak, when his

beeper went off. He ignored it, but it went off again and then again.

"Damn," he muttered. "I've got to call the station. I'll be back in a second."

Relief washed over her face at the reprieve.

"I will be back, though, and we will finish this conversation," he vowed as he went toward the pay phone to call the station.

Justin quickly placed a call to the station. "Justin, I'm sorry to call you, but I thought you'd want to know," the late-night dispatcher said.

"What? Couldn't it wait until morning?" he asked impatiently.

"There's been an accident on the highway coming into town from White Pines. It's Sharon Lynn and Kyle."

Cold dread settled in the pit of his stomach. "Are they okay?"

"It's bad, Justin. Real bad. I think you'd better get out there."

He slammed the phone down and walked slowly back to the table. "I have to go," he said, his voice cracking on a sob he hadn't even known was bottled up inside.

Patsy jumped up and followed him. "Justin? What is it? You're white as a ghost."

"An accident," he said. "Sharon Lynn and Kyle."

All of the color drained out of her face, too. "I'm coming with you."

"No. There's no need. I can drop you at your place."

Her chin shot up. "I'm coming with you," she repeated. "Are you going to waste time standing here arguing?"

He realized then how desperately he wanted her with him, how very badly he would need her to hang on to if the news was as grim as the dispatcher had made it sound.

"Buckle up, then," he said grimly as she climbed into the car and shot him a look that dared him to argue.

"You won't help anyone by getting killed en route," she said softly as he took the corner on two wheels and shot down Main Street.

He slowed, but only to the point of reason and well in excess of the speed limit. He'd done enough training and high-speed chases to know precisely what his own limits were on the road. He drove with total concentration, allowing his mind to wander only long enough to utter a few fervent prayers that Sharon Lynn and her new husband would be all right.

What in God's name had happened? Kyle was a good driver, the roads were practically deserted this time of night and he'd bet the ranch that neither of them had had more than a glass of champagne during the reception.

"I see the flashing lights up ahead," Patsy murmured, fear in her voice. "It looks as if there's a lot of them."

"That just means they're getting all the help they need. Nothing to panic over." He said it as much for his own benefit as hers.

They arrived just as an ambulance sped off toward Garden City in the opposite direction, siren blaring. There were two more on the scene and paramedics seemed to be everywhere, most of them volunteers who'd come scrambling in pickups, lights flashing on their dashboards and casting an eerie glow in the dark.

A huge spotlight was shining on the twisted wreckage of Kyle's car, guiding him through the maze of rescue vehicles, police cars and ambulances. One glimpse was enough to make Justin want to retch. He heard Patsy's gasp beside him at the sight of the crushed passenger compartment.

"Get back into the car," he said. "There's nothing you can do to help. I'll find out what's happening."

"Sharon Lynn," she began in a whisper every bit as tormented as his own thoughts.

"Shh, don't think the worst. Let me get some answers."

He herded her back toward his car, then moved again through the tangle of debris and people. He saw the expressions of sympathy and knew then that the news wasn't going to be good.

Swallowing hard, he forced himself to face the deputy in charge. "My cousin," he began. It was all he could say without falling apart.

"Sharon Lynn's badly injured, but she's going to make it," Dusty assured him. "She's unconscious, but her vital signs were good. She's already on her way to the hospital."

Justin's gaze was drawn back to the collapsed mass of metal on the passenger side. "But how?"

"She was driving," Dusty said succinctly. "The air bag saved her. Kyle took the brunt of the impact." He looked as if he wanted to cry, too. "He…he wasn't so lucky, Justin. There was a faint pulse when we got here, but we couldn't get him out in time to save him. The guys did everything they could."

Justin felt the world begin to spin. Sheer will kept him upright. "Do you know what happened?"

"A drunk crossed the center line. It looked as if Sharon Lynn tried to get out of his way, but with no shoulders and those deep ditches, there was no place to go."

"Is he dead?"

Dusty looked startled that he cared. "The drunk driver?"

Justin nodded.

"No, he's over there. Some minor cuts and bruises. He'll walk away."

Pure rage made Justin see red. He turned in the direction the deputy had indicated, ignoring Dusty's commands to stop, to let it go. He had to see for himself, had to look into the face of the man who'd murdered his cousin's husband, who'd almost killed her, as well.

And then he might very well beat that face into a bloody pulp.

Chapter Nine

Patsy saw Justin walking toward the side of the highway. There was something about his jerky, dazed progress that brought her scrambling from the car and heading straight for him. She reached him just as a deputy she recognized as Dusty Patterson got to his side and clamped a hand on his shoulder.

"Get away from me," Justin demanded, his voice like ice.

"Don't do this," Dusty pleaded. "You're not thinking straight."

Anger radiated from Justin in palpable waves. Even without knowing what was going on, Patsy sensed that he was about to do something he would come to regret. Instinctively she stepped in front of the two men.

"Justin?"

When he didn't even glance at her, she spoke his name again, more sharply this time. As if he'd been drawn out of some distant hell, his gaze finally shifted to clash with hers. The sight of the tears streaking down his cheeks was almost her undoing. There was no doubt in her mind now that something truly terrible had happened to Sharon Lynn and Kyle. What else could create such despair in such a strong man?

She reached up and touched his face. "Come with me, please," she begged.

For the longest time, she wasn't sure he would agree. He seemed torn between anger and a distress so deep and heart wrenching, she could only fear its cause. At last, he turned away and went with her.

He got into the car and leaned forward, his head resting on the steering wheel. Quiet sobs shook his shoulders. Patsy scrambled across the seat and put her arms around him. As desperately as she wanted to know what had happened, how badly Kyle and Sharon Lynn were injured, she kept silent, letting Justin do his grieving in silence while she fought her own fears.

It seemed they remained like that forever, but in truth it was no more than a minute or two, she realized, before he drew in a shuddering breath and faced her.

"We have to go to the hospital."

"Sharon Lynn and Kyle are there?"

He shook his head. "Only Sharon Lynn."

The implication of that tore through her. "Oh, my God. Kyle?"

"Didn't make it." He looked so shattered that all she wanted to do was reach over and hold him again, but he was already starting the engine. The grim set of his mouth told her he wouldn't appreciate a show of sympathy right now, that he'd only tolerated the first display because he'd been nearly oblivious to it. All she could do was stay with him, be there when he needed someone and be there for Sharon Lynn, whose world had just come crashing down around her head. She thought of Sharon Lynn's terrible premonition that her future with Kyle was jinxed and realized the enormity of what lay ahead for her.

At the hospital, they found the rest of the family already gathered, most of them still in the clothes they'd worn to the wedding. Patsy faded into the background once she was certain that Justin was being taken care of by his family.

She wandered from the emergency room waiting area and went in search of a chapel. When she found it off the main lobby, she went inside and found Janet Adams already there, her face damp with tears.

Patsy started to tiptoe out again, but the older woman spotted her and held out her hand. "Come, sit with me. I just came to tell God how grateful we are for sparing Sharon Lynn."

"What about how angry we are that Kyle was taken from her?" Patsy asked, unable to hide her own bitterness on her friend's behalf. "How could this happen to someone as decent and kind as Sharon Lynn?''

''God never gives us any pain he doesn't think will make us stronger.''

Patsy wondered about that. Then she thought of her own life up until now. When she'd been caught up in Will's web of snide remarks and psychological abuse, she'd thought only about the terrible sense of failure he was instilling in her. When she'd run, she'd felt more like a victim than ever and she'd cursed him for that, hating him every bit as much as if he'd hit her.

But she was stronger now and her strength had come out of that pain. Would the same be true for Sharon Lynn? She could only pray that Janet was right.

They sat quietly side by side, lost in their own thoughts, taking comfort from each other's presence. It was a long time before she looked up and saw Justin standing hesitantly in the doorway. ''I heard this was where you'd gone,'' he said, still not coming into the quiet, dimly lit chapel.

Janet regarded him with sympathy. ''I'm sorry you had to be there tonight. It must have been terrible for you.''

Anger flashed in his eyes. ''I'm not the one who needs your pity. Save it for Sharon Lynn. I only wish I could have killed the man responsible when I had the chance.''

''You don't mean that,'' Janet said gently. ''The courts will hand down justice. It wasn't up to you. You know that's the way it has to be.''

"Do I?" he asked bitterly. His gaze shifted to Patsy. "There's nothing more we can do here tonight. I'll take you home."

She nodded and squeezed Janet's hand. "Thank you for what you said. It meant a lot to me. If there's anything I can do for any of you, let me know."

Janet glanced toward the doorway. "Stay with Justin," she said, her expression worried. "He's going to need you. You heard him just now. This doesn't fit with his sense of justice at all. It won't be easy for him to reconcile it." She sighed. "If I'm being totally honest, no matter what I said before, even I know it won't be easy for any of us."

The next few days went by in a terrible haze. Patsy did the only thing she could think of to do that might help. She kept the lunch counter at Dolan's running smoothly from dawn to dusk. The news on Sharon Lynn was more positive each day and by the beginning of the following week she had been released from the hospital. Patsy went to visit her at the ranch, where the whole family was hovering over her. When she went into Sharon Lynn's room, she was horrified by what she found.

Though Sharon Lynn's injuries were healing nicely and the bruises had begun to fade, she was lying in bed staring dully at the ceiling. When Patsy had walked into the room, her friend had not even glanced in her direction.

"Hey," Patsy said softly. "I'm so relieved to see you safe at home again."

Sharon Lynn nodded, her expression blank. ''Thanks,'' she murmured with no emotion in her voice at all.

''Everyone at Dolan's misses you like crazy. They're asking when you'll be back.''

No response. Patsy tried again.

''What is the doctor saying about getting back on your feet again?''

''Not much.''

Patsy didn't know too much about clinical depression, but it seemed to her that Sharon Lynn was sinking into the kind of dark despair that needed quick attention. She wondered if anyone had broached the subject with her, then wondered if she dared do it herself. She was still debating whether she had any right or even an obligation to say something, when Sharon Lynn spoke.

''I killed him, you know.'' She whispered it matter-of-factly.

Patsy reacted angrily. ''Don't be absurd. Kyle was killed by a drunk driver. Don't you ever think otherwise.''

''But I was driving our car. I should have done...'' Her voice trailed off before she finally added forlornly, ''Something. I should have done something.''

Patsy reached for her hand. It was ice-cold and limp. ''There was nothing you could have done, no place you could turn,'' she insisted. ''The road's narrow, and there are deep ditches on either side. The only person responsible for this tragedy was the other driver.''

The door to the room opened just as she spoke.

"Damn right!" Justin said fiercely. He came over to the bed and reached down for Sharon Lynn's hand. "Don't you dare blame yourself. The slime who did this should be locked up for a long, long time. The sheriff will see that he is."

Sharon Lynn retreated visibly, staring back up at the ceiling again, her expression blank. Patsy beckoned to Justin and led him from the room. It was the first time she'd seen him in days as well. He looked only marginally better than his cousin. She wanted to throw her arms around him and hold him. It was a strange feeling to think of herself as the strong one after so many years of believing herself to be weak.

"Are you okay?" she asked quietly.

A ghost of a smile came and went. "Better now that I've seen you."

"You don't look as if you've slept a wink in days."

"You mean I'm not as handsome as ever?" he asked, a twinkle bringing a momentary light to his eyes.

"Oh, you'll always be handsome enough, Justin Adams, but right now you're pale and drawn. Haven't you been eating? You haven't been by Dolan's since this happened."

He did smile at that. "Did you miss me?"

"Of course not. I just worried that the thieves were going to start getting ideas now that there hasn't been a lawman parked at the counter for days."

"So it's my badge you've been missing," he

teased. "I'm surprised. I always had the feeling it made you nervous."

Patsy's pulse thudded dully at the taunt. It was too close to being squarely on the mark.

"I don't hear you denying it," he said.

"Because it's so ridiculous it doesn't deserve a reply," she said, trying to brazen it out. She met his gaze unblinkingly.

Eventually he grinned. "If you say so, darlin'."

"Can we talk about Sharon Lynn for a minute?" she asked.

She knew it was a topic that would fully capture his attention and get the glare of the spotlight off her for a bit. As she'd anticipated, a worried frown creased his brow.

"What about her?"

"I think maybe she's going to need some help getting through this."

"She's getting help. We're all here. All she has to do is say the word and any one of us will get her whatever she needs."

"I'm not talking about soup or some custard when she says she's hungry. I'm talking about professional help."

"A shrink?"

She nodded.

"That's crazy," he said indignantly. "Anyone would be upset after a tragedy like this. Sharon Lynn's strong. She's an Adams. She'll pull herself together in time."

Patsy was doubtful. "Will she? She's eaten up with

guilt. She told me she killed Kyle. You heard her yourself.''

''That's the grief talking. She'll put this into perspective. Once the other driver is convicted and locked away, she'll see it wasn't her fault.''

Patsy remained silent in response. Finally Justin said, ''You don't believe that, do you?''

''No, I don't. There's something about the way she's staring off into space, as if she's slowly disconnecting from the world. It worries me. Maybe it's just grief, but it seems to me it goes deeper than that. It's not just that she's lost Kyle.'' She struggled to put it into words. ''It's as if she's lost her reason for living.''

''And you got all that from a five-minute visit?'' Justin asked, his expression incredulous.

Patsy refused to back down, even in the face of his blatant skepticism. ''Okay, it's just my opinion and I'm not an expert. I'm just saying an expert would be able to say once and for all if she needs some counseling. Don't trust my judgment, just ask yourself if you want to take the chance that I'm right.''

Justin sighed and ran his fingers through his close-cropped hair. ''Hell, I suppose you could be right. It's just that Adamses solve their own problems.''

''Sometimes the solution is asking for help,'' Patsy said.

''I'll mention it to the family and see what they think,'' Justin promised. He reached over and tucked a stray curl behind her ear. ''By the way, has anyone thanked you for pitching in and taking over at Dolan's?''

''I don't need to be thanked. It's my job. Dani's staff has been great about helping with Billy so I could be there longer hours.''

''Don't work yourself to a frazzle,'' he warned. ''You need to look after yourself, too.''

She gazed into his eyes and saw genuine concern there. It was the first time in as long as she could remember that anyone had been truly worried about her well-being. It had mattered to Will only as far as her ability to campaign on his behalf.

''I'm fine,'' she reassured Justin. ''But I'd better be getting back into town. With the hours I'm putting in at Dolan's, I don't like to leave Billy with a sitter in the evenings, too.''

''Mind if I come along?'' Justin asked. ''I promised him I'd be by to play with those toys we bought. I haven't had a chance up until now. Frankly, I could use a break from all this.''

''He'd like that.''

''And you? Would you like that, too?''

She knew what he was really asking, but she wasn't sure she entirely trusted his motives. Did it really matter to him whether she was beginning to care for him or was he simply trying to test her again? Even though it had been days since their last talk and despite all that had happened, she doubted Justin had forgotten all the questions he had about her past.

''Of course,'' she said cheerily. ''If you haven't eaten yet, you can share a pizza with us.''

"Why don't I pick it up on my way and meet you at the house?"

"I can do it."

"Why should you when I can and you can get home to Billy that much sooner?"

She grinned. "Okay, when you put it like that, how can I argue? But I insist on paying for it."

"We'll discuss that later."

"Justin!" She took a twenty from her purse and tried to press it into his hands. He jammed his hands into his pockets and defied her to follow with the money. She was tempted to do just that, but the prospect of finding her own hand trapped between his and his body with only a layer of denim in between rattled her too badly. That jittery temptation was proof enough that she had no business getting in any kind of intimate contact with him.

She sighed. "Okay, you win. We'll discuss it later."

He grinned. "It's nice to see that you can compromise."

"Is that what you call it?"

"Sure, darlin'. I have it on the best authority that compromise is very important in any relationship."

Patsy didn't know whether to cheer or turn tail and run at the mention of the word *relationship*. She and Justin weren't having a relationship. It was impossible.

But, oh, how she wished it weren't.

"Patsy?"

Startled, she glanced up and met Justin's worried frown.

"Everything okay?"

"Sure," she lied. "Just trying to remember how big a mess the house is in. I'd hate for you to walk in and wonder if a tornado blew through. After all, it is your sister's place. I'd hate to have her evict me."

"There's no chance of that," he assured her. "And don't worry about the state of your housekeeping. With all the nieces and nephews running around in this family, no one knows the meaning of tidy anymore."

"Not even you? You live alone and, as I recall, your place was spotless the one time I came over."

"That's because I'm never there. And it's not tidy. It's sterile. Give me chaos any day. It's what makes the difference between a house and a home."

"Maybe I should let Billy come and visit for an afternoon. The resulting mess ought to send you into raptures."

"I'd love it," he said, much to her amazement. "In the meantime, let's get into town. Suddenly I'm starved for the first time in days."

The gleam in his eyes was a reminder that food was not the only thing a man could be starved for. Patsy was drawn to that look, wanted desperately to respond to it, but decency prevented it.

She had the whole long drive into town to wonder how long she could allow this marital limbo to drag on. It was unfair to Billy and to her. Maybe even to

Will. Most of all, though, it was unfair to Justin, because he didn't even know what he was up against.

How was she going to resolve it? Could she simply file for divorce long-distance and pray that Will went along with it? Thinking he would was a foolish idea. He was a very possessive man. Even though she knew he no longer loved her—if he ever had—he would fight the divorce if only because he would fear the damage to his image if he let her go. He would demand custody of Billy for the same reason.

Her feet were dragging as she walked into the house, not just from exhaustion, but from despair. How could she ever truly move on with her life, build a real future for herself and her son, unless she resolved things with Will? She'd been crazy to think that simply running away would solve all of her problems. It had removed her and Billy from harm's way, but it had created a whole new set of problems.

Still the thought of seeing Will again under any circumstances terrified her. She had weathered a lot in the past couple of months. She was far stronger than she'd been when she'd run from Oklahoma, but was she strong enough for the battle that was likely to ensue?

Before she could reach any conclusion at all about that, Billy came running toward her, arms held high, a piece of paper clutched in one tiny hand.

"Mama, Mama, Mama," he chanted. "Me drew picture for you. See?"

She took the paper and looked at the colorful scribbles. They were meaningless to her, but clearly not to her son. She hunkered down beside him. "This is beautiful," she said admiringly. "Tell me about it."

"I drewed us. We're a family. See?" He pointed to the littlest batch of swirls and lines. "That's me. And that's you."

"Ah," she said, seeing the relative difference in sizes, if not the identifying details. "And this?"

"That's Daddy." There was a mulish lift to his chin when he said it, then added, "Want to see Daddy."

"Daddy's far away," she reminded him.

"Want to see him."

"Maybe we can call him later."

"Now," Billy demanded. "Call now."

Patsy sighed. She had promised him days ago that they would call his daddy, but there had never been time to take a trip to some out-of-the-way pay phone that couldn't be traced. Obviously she would have to make the time.

"Tomorrow," she promised. She would get one of the women who'd volunteered to help out at Dolan's in Sharon Lynn's absence to fill in long enough for her to take Billy to make the phone call. "Now why don't we get you cleaned up? Justin's coming over and he's bringing pizza."

The mention of his favorite food—to say nothing of his favorite grown-up playmate—was enough to distract him. She went into the living room where Flo Bartle was waiting. Flo lived next door and, since the accident, had taken over baby-sitting duty when Dani's staff left for the day.

"Flo, I can't thank you enough for looking out for Billy for me."

"No problem. He's an angel. You do whatever you need to do to help out Sharon Lynn. There are plenty of us who can pitch in and help with Billy. All I'd be doing at home is watching my husband snooze through the national news. Believe me, I'd rather be here."

"Justin's bringing a pizza by. Would you like to stay?"

"No, indeed. I'd have heartburn the rest of the night." She winked. "Besides, I doubt Justin's coming by so he can look at an old lady across the table."

"It would be fine," Patsy insisted. "Justin and I are just friends."

"If you say so, dear. Just remember there are friends and then there are *friends*."

"Hey, Mrs. B.," Justin called out as he came up the walk carrying a huge pizza box. "You get more beautiful every time I see you."

"Then your eyesight's going, boy, or else you're as full of blarney as every other male in your family."

He dropped a kiss on her cheek. "I'm a deputy sheriff, Mrs. B. I'm sworn to uphold the law and to tell the truth, so help me God."

The teasing comment put a sparkle in her neighbor's eyes, but it sent a shiver down Patsy's spine. Once again she'd been reminded of the position she'd been putting Justin in since the day they'd met. It had to stop.

Tomorrow, she vowed to herself as she had to Billy

earlier. Tomorrow, when she called Will, she would test the waters and see if there was any way to put an end to all the lies and deception or whether she was doomed to a life in limbo.

Chapter Ten

It was the first time since the night of the accident that Justin had let himself relax. He was stretched out on the floor in Patsy's living room, his back braced against the sofa, the empty pizza box off to one side, as he watched Billy struggle to build a tower with a new set of blocks.

One block, two, then eventually six, stacked in a way that virtually assured disaster. With awkward fingers Billy tried to put the seventh block on top, only to set the whole stack to teetering dangerously. Justin reached over and steadied it, but balance was elusive. It toppled over, sending Billy into fits of giggles.

"Again," he insisted, putting the first block into place.

"Maybe it needs a bigger base," Justin suggested idly.

"What's a base?" Billy demanded.

"More blocks on the bottom." He reached over and set four of the colorful plastic blocks into a square, then stacked two on top of that. "See, like this."

"Won't fall down?" Billy asked skeptically.

"Nope."

"'Kay," Billy agreed, and added another block to the pile, then another.

When it all teetered and fell again, he stared at it with a look of such betrayal in his eyes that Justin felt like a heel. This time tears, rather than giggles, accompanied the architectural disaster.

"Maybe I'm not as good an engineer as I thought," he apologized.

"Or maybe your work crew isn't past the apprentice stage yet," Patsy suggested, grinning at them. "It's Billy's bedtime, anyway."

"No," Billy said at once, even though his eyelids had been drooping for the past half hour.

"I'll put you to bed and tell you a story," Justin offered.

Billy's eyes widened. "You will?"

"Indeed, I will. I'll tell you the story about a girl named Little Red Riding Hood and this big, bad wolf."

"No. Want rabbit story."

Justin shrugged. "Then the rabbit story it will be, but I gotta tell you, kid, the big, bad wolf is much more of a guy thing."

"He might be a little young for guy things," Patsy

said, her expression amused. "And you won't be the one left to deal with the nightmares."

"Okay, Mom. I bow to your superior knowledge on the subject," he said, scooping Billy up and tickling him until he giggled. The sound was pure delight, so he kept it up. It reminded him of things like innocence and simple pleasures. It reminded him of all the things he wanted and that were out of reach.

"You realize, of course, that if you do that much more he'll never get to sleep," Patsy observed.

Justin shook his head and gave Billy a sympathetic look. "Moms just don't get it, do they?"

Billy shook his head. "Don't get it."

He carried Billy into his room and helped him into his pj's, then settled him in bed. He'd done the same thing a hundred times with his nieces and nephews, but there was something different about putting Billy to bed. The kids in his family all had adoring dads of their own. He was just a welcome variance in their routine. With Billy he sensed that having a man put him to bed was a whole new experience. He seemed wide-eyed that Justin would want to, and pitifully eager to prolong the storytelling as long as possible.

"Read it again," he begged, even though he could barely hold his eyes open after the second time.

"Close your eyes and go to sleep," Justin countered. "I'll read for five more minutes, but you'd better be snoozing when I'm done."

Billy smiled contentedly and snuggled down beneath the covers. He dutifully closed his eyes. As Justin had expected, he was sound asleep before Justin had finished reading the first page. Justin sat for a moment longer and stared at the boy, amazed by the sense of yearning that came over him.

Why had he waited so long before claiming nights like this for himself? He'd been dating forever—maybe not as extensively as Harlan Patrick, but enthusiastically. The idea of settling down had never once crossed his mind until now.

He sighed heavily. It would have to be a woman with secrets and a boy with coal black eyes who drew him. Something told him that down that path lay heartache. The new report that had landed on Tate's desk today confirmed it. Will Longhorn was now claiming that Patsy had kidnapped their son. The stakes had escalated way past his own needs and longings.

He was still sitting there when he sensed Patsy behind him. He jolted when her hand came to rest on his shoulder. The touch was as light and tentative as the flutter of a bird's wings, but he felt as if it were the most intimate caress he'd ever shared.

"You guys finish your story?" she whispered.

"Twice," he admitted.

"Dani was right. He does have you wound around his little finger. I thought you were made of tougher stuff than that."

"He gets to me."

"Why?"

He shrugged. "I'm not sure. Is it possible for a man to feel an instinctive bond with a child who's not his own?"

"Adoptive dads do that all the time."

"True." He glanced over his shoulder into her eyes. "Maybe I'm just getting to a time in my life when I'm thinking about a family and wondering when I'll have one of my own."

"You will when you want to," she said. "You come from a long line of men who go after whatever they want. They're all family men, with deep roots. You're no different."

"What happens if I pick the wrong woman?" he inquired softly, meeting her gaze evenly. "What if I pick someone who's not free to love me back?"

He saw the flare of alarm in her eyes, the sudden rush of dismay that stripped the color from her cheeks.

"What are you saying?" she asked, her voice shaky.

He refused to look away or to yield to her obvious panic. "I'm just wondering, hypothetically, what would happen to my dreams if I fell in love with a woman who's not available? Where would that leave me?"

Rather than answer, she whirled and left the room. Justin followed slowly. He found her on the front porch, staring out at the night sky. He walked up behind her and rested his hands on her shoulders, much as she had done to him earlier. He could feel her trembling, felt the buck of her pulse where his thumb rested against her neck.

And then he felt the hot splash of a tear on his hand. It almost brought him to his knees. He hadn't meant for her to cry, hadn't meant to shake her so badly that she would run from him. He'd just wanted to prod her into opening up at last. Maybe a direct, straightforward question would have been better, after all.

He turned her gently, then pulled her into his arms. She resisted for no more than a heartbeat, then rested her head against his shoulder.

"I'm sorry," he apologized.

"For what?"

"Pushing again."

"It's not that."

"What then?"

She drew in a deep, shuddering breath, then whispered, "You know, don't you? I've sensed it for days now."

His own breath caught in his throat. At last, he thought. At last there would be truth between them.

And then what? he wondered to himself. What the hell would he do when the truth was out? There would be no turning back, then. What if it started them both down a path that destroyed any hope of the future he'd been envisioning just a short time before?

"Know what?" he asked, because he had to, because it was the only thing to do. The kidnapping charge was too serious to be ignored, no matter how ridiculous he might believe it to be. "About me." She drew in a deep breath, then blurted, "That I'm married."

He sighed. He'd hoped, prayed, that he'd been

wrong about that, that she was divorced at least, but the report on Tate's desk hadn't lied. Will Longhorn was still her husband. What was the rest of the truth, though? Were they in the process of getting a divorce? Was there a battle for custody? Had she kidnapped their son to avoid losing him to her husband? Justin didn't believe that, even though it would explain the skittishness, the use of her maiden name, rather than her husband's. He would lay odds that she had every right to have that boy with her.

"Maybe I'm the wrong person for you to talk to about this," he said finally.

She regarded him incredulously. "You forced this into the open and now you don't want to talk about it?"

He touched a silencing finger to her lips. "It's not that I don't want to hear everything. I just think maybe it would be best if you talked to Janet."

"Why?"

"Because she's an attorney and a damned fine one. If you're in trouble, she can help. She'll want to, you know that. You won't go wrong listening to her."

"Who says I need an attorney?"

"I do," he said, a gentle hand on her cheek. "Listen to me. Talk to Janet."

"Justin, how much do you know?"

"Not everything," he admitted. "I know that your husband is looking for you."

She sighed. "I thought he might be. What else?"

"He's accusing you of kidnapping your baby."

She stared at him in shock. "Kidnapping? That's

absurd. Billy is mine as much as he is Will's. There's been no divorce, no custody battle. There's no way he could accuse me of kidnapping my own son.'' She regarded him with a panicky expression. ''Could he?''

He rushed to reassure her. ''He can make all the accusations he wants, but it remains to be seen if any of them will stand up in court. That's why I think you should talk to Janet.''

''I can't,'' she whispered. ''What if she says I have to go back? What if she tells me he can take Billy away from me, that I have to give up my son?''

He studied her intently, recognizing the genuine fear in her eyes. ''Has Will Longhorn ever hurt you?''

His heart was in his throat as he waited what seemed to be a lifetime for her to slowly shake her head.

''Not physically, no. He's come close. His temper gets out of control. He's threatened me, my parents. It was terrifyingly real.''

And then she burst into tears and buried her face in her hands. All Justin could do was wait out the storm, his arms around her, his shirt growing damp with her tears. Eventually, when the sobs subsided, he handed her a handkerchief. She blotted her eyes and scrubbed away the dampness on her cheeks.

''I'm sorry.''

''There's nothing to apologize for,'' he insisted.

Patsy sighed heavily. ''I knew I should have dealt with this straight on, but I was so afraid, Justin. I was afraid he'd take my baby. That's what he threatened to do.''

Once the words were out, it was as if a dam had burst. She told him everything, about meeting the attractive, ambitious young attorney, about working for him and falling in love, about marrying him and joining him in his political rise, only to have their home life disintegrate.

''I was his trophy wife, the all-American girl. I know it wasn't true, but sometimes I wondered if he hadn't married me because his political advisers told him to. He resented me that much.''

Justin heard pain and confusion in her voice, but not the bitterness he'd expected. That was a surprise. He touched a hand to her cheek. ''Are you still in love with him?''

She stared at him in shock. ''In love with Will? No. He killed whatever love there was between us a long time ago.''

Relief washed over him. He'd had to be sure. If there was even a lingering trace of love for the man back in Oklahoma, then his advice might have been different. Instead, he advised one more time. ''Talk to Janet. She will tell you what your legal options are.''

''I'll think about it,'' she promised.

''Do it,'' he said more sharply than he'd intended. He sighed. ''Sorry. It's just that I can't bury these notices forever and neither can Tate.''

She stared at him, her expression horrified. ''Tate knows?''

Justin nodded. "He found the first report. He's left it up to me to take care of this for the moment, but it can't wait forever. Earlier today it escalated from a simple missing persons report to a kidnapping charge. It sounds as if your husband's getting desperate."

"I've put you in a terrible position, haven't I?"

He noticed that she put concern for him ahead of concern for her husband. That was something to hold on to in the days ahead. There was no question it was going to get messy. Any man who would threaten his wife with violence as Will Longhorn had was dangerous. He was also a lawyer with political connections. It was impossible to tell what lengths he might go to before everything was sorted out in a courtroom.

"I want you to think about moving out to White Pines," he said carefully. "Billy will have a wonderful time on the ranch and there will be people around."

"You think this is going to get ugly, don't you?"

"Hasn't it already?" he asked dryly.

"But I can't involve your family. It's bad enough that you're in the middle of this."

"I made the choice," he said. "I could have called the Oklahoma authorities the second I knew who you were. So could Tate."

"Why didn't you?"

His mouth curved slowly. "Darlin', if you don't know that, then you're not half as quick as I've been giving you credit for being."

A faint smile touched her lips, then faded just as quickly. "And Tate?"

"Tate's a lot like Grandpa Harlan. He's the kind of a man who trusts his gut instincts. And when it comes to a choice between that and a piece of paper coming in over a fax machine, he'll go with his gut every time. He likes you. He believes there's more to the story than what's on those papers and until his back's to the wall, he'll do everything he can to protect you. In the meantime, I'd feel a whole lot better if you were out at White Pines."

"I can't impose like that, especially not if things start getting ugly."

"That's exactly why you need to be there. Grandpa Harlan will stand up to the devil himself to protect those he loves. Cody's there and Harlan Patrick, not that I want you seeing too much of him."

"No," she said, that familiar stubborn tilt to her chin. "This is my fight, not your family's."

He regarded her soberly. "I'm making it mine."

"No," she said again, though a little less forcefully.

Justin grinned. "Yes. Don't fight me on this, darlin'. My mind's made up and nobody on earth's more stubborn than an Adams."

"We could debate that," she teased, her expression brightening for the first time since the conversation began. "I'm not exactly a pushover."

"No, you are anything but a pushover," he agreed, amused. "Let's just say you've met your match."

He'd made the remark lightly, but the words hung in the air and set off a sizzling tension. Patsy's gaze locked with his.

"Yes," she said very quietly. "I think maybe I have."

After that soft-spoken admission, it took every last bit of willpower Justin possessed to walk away from her and go back to his own place. It was late. He was exhausted. Stress piled on top of stress for days now had left him thoroughly drained. And yet he knew he wouldn't sleep.

He was a man who liked to control his own destiny and too much of his future hinged now on other people. For the first time since he'd put on a badge he regretted it. It kept him from being able to track down Will Longhorn and bloody his nose for the hell he'd put Patsy through and the likely anguish that was yet to come.

Even with right on her side, there was no way to be sure that things wouldn't get twisted around in a courtroom with Patsy coming out the loser. That was why she needed Janet at the moment, even more than she needed him. He could love her—and God knows he'd finally recognized that he did—but he couldn't protect her from the fallout of her own impetuous decision to run. Not that he blamed her for not wanting to square off against her husband when all the odds were stacked in his favor.

That, at least, was no longer true. With the considerable force of the Adams name behind her now, Patsy stood a better than even chance in a legal battle.

But what if she lost? He had to consider that possibility. Nothing was certain when it came to the whims of judges. He'd seen too many black-and-white cases dismissed on a technicality. He had to believe, though, that she would win. If she didn't, then nothing he worked for as a law enforcement officer was worth anything.

If the legal system went awry, what then? What if he was forced to choose between a misguided legal decision and what he saw as Patsy's God-given right to have her son? God help him, what would he do? Encourage her to take Billy and run again? Go with them, leaving behind his family, his principles?

It won't come to that, he reassured himself time and again. It would be too cruel.

But fate could take cruel twists. Just ask Sharon Lynn. She'd waited for years to finally marry the man she loved, only to lose him on her wedding night. Where was the justice in that?

He thought back to those few brief hours earlier in the evening when he'd actually felt at ease for the first time in days. Why the devil had he insisted on opening up this whole blasted can of worms? Maybe ignorance really was bliss. A few hours ago he'd only suspected the tangle of problems facing Patsy. Now he knew for sure what was ahead of her, ahead of both of them.

How could he possibly seize control of this before things got out of hand? Other than pounding some sense into Will Longhorn, that is? Longhorn held the answers, though. And Justin was a cop with all sorts of investigative skills at his command.

His spirits brightened. Maybe he couldn't do anything officially, but unofficially? Yes, indeed, he could find out if there was so much as a parking violation outstanding in the man's past. If there was anything, anything at all, he would hand it to Patsy and Janet as ammunition for the battle ahead.

With something concrete he could do to help Patsy, his mind eased and he finally fell into a deep sleep. Unfortunately, it lasted little more than half an hour before the alarm was going off and the phone was ringing.

"Justin, I'm sorry to wake you," Becky apologized. "But you'd better get over to Dolan's right away."

He struggled to shake the cobwebs from his mind. "Dolan's? Why? What's happened?"

"Patsy just called. She was too upset for me to make much sense of it, but I think she said someone's trying to break down the front door."

He glanced at the clock. Patsy wasn't due at work for another half hour. "She's there?"

"Locked in the back room is what she said. I could hear the glass breaking."

"I'm on my way. Have you called Tate?"

"Not yet. I got Dusty rolling first. He was just coming back into town from a patrol on the highway. He's on his way. Should be there any second now."

"I'm on my way," he said, and hung up. He was still pulling on his clothes as he ran out of the house. He had his service revolver tucked into his waistband.

It took him less than five minutes to reach Main Street. He could hear the commotion as he made the turn. Glass was shattering and someone was laying into whatever remained of the front of the store with something heavy, more than likely a crowbar or tire iron. Dusty was shouting commands that were being ignored. Instead, more debris flew, amid a flurry of curses and threats.

Justin made the turn on two wheels, then slammed to a stop behind Dusty's patrol car. He stared at the mess in disbelief.

"What the hell's going on?"

Dusty turned, his expression shaken. "Beats the hell out of me. Looks like the guy just lost it. Either he's got a grudge against Doc or he's a junkie out of his mind and desperate for drugs. Do you recognize him?"

Justin surveyed the man, from his pitch-dark black hair to his sculpted cheekbones, angled jaw and well-tailored suit. This was no thug or drifter. In fact, he concluded with a sinking heart, he would bet the ranch that this was Will Longhorn. He glanced up and down the block until he spotted a very fancy car that was almost exactly like Patsy's, just shiny black to her white one.

"Can you see the tags on that car?" he asked Dusty, who had a better angle on them.

"Oklahoma."

"Damn."

"What the hell is going on here?" Tate demanded, joining them.

"Unless I miss my guess, we're about to meet Will Longhorn," Justin said.

Tate's eyebrows rose. "Patsy's husband?"

"The one and only. It appears he's come calling, though I have to say his courting leaves a little something to be desired."

The sheriff's expression cheered considerably. "Well, well, well. It will surely be my pleasure to lock him up." He glanced at Justin and Dusty. "Shall we?"

"Oh, yeah," Justin said grimly.

Tate gave him a sharp look. "You don't lay a hand on him. Understood?"

Justin grimaced, then sighed. "Yes, sir."

"Then let's do it," Tate said.

It was an uneven fight, three against one with the three armed, as well. Tate had slapped handcuffs on the man before he even realized he was being taken into custody. When he heard the click and felt the cold metal around his wrists, he whirled on Tate.

"What the hell do you think you're doing?"

"Arresting you," Tate said evenly. "We can start with destruction of property and go from there." He began reading him his rights.

"Do you know who I am?"

"I don't give a damn if you're the governor or the president of the U.S. of A., nobody pulls a stunt like this in my town," Tate retorted.

Justin didn't waste time listening to the rest of the exchange. He stepped over glass shards and broken toys from the window displays, then used his own key to the drugstore. As he went inside, he called out to Patsy. The door to the back room cracked open.

"Justin?"

"It's me," he said, and opened his arms.

Patsy ran straight into them and clung. "Oh, my God, did you see him? He's lost his mind. He must have."

"I take it that's Will."

Her head bobbed against his chest.

"It's okay, darlin'. Tate has him in custody. He won't hurt you."

"But this place," she murmured, gazing around in horror. "Look what he's done."

"As long as you're all right, it doesn't matter. We'll have it cleaned up in no time."

"I can't believe this. It's all my fault."

"It is not your fault," Justin said. "He's an adult. He's responsible for his own actions, and believe me, this is not going to look good when you go into court and ask for your divorce. You have three cops as witnesses to the violence he's capable of. You can't get any better than that."

Patsy regarded him sadly. "It won't be that easy. He won't let it be."

"I know. But I'll be right here with you." He tilted her chin up and gazed into her eyes. "Believe it or not, this is a good thing."

She stared at the broken glass and demolished displays. "You'll pardon me if I can't quite see it that way."

"Darlin', I think I could forgive you just about anything. Now get a couple of brooms and let's get busy."

"Don't you have to go down to the station?"

"Not yet. Tate can handle your husband. When things settle down a bit, you and I can go down there and you can press formal charges against him. Doc Dolan can press whatever charges he wants to for the damage to the store. Then you can see Janet and we'll find out just what kind of a case she can put together for you." He brushed a wayward curl from her cheek. "It's almost over, Patsy. I guarantee it."

But, of course, it was just beginning.

Chapter Eleven

The last place on earth Patsy wanted to be was the sheriff's office. Even with Justin by her side, she dreaded confronting Will after the scene and destruction he'd caused. She was thoroughly embarrassed, not only for herself, but for him. He'd always been such a proud person. She didn't like thinking that she was to blame for him being reduced to this out-of-control mockery of a man.

"Want me to come in with you?" Justin asked as she hesitated at the doorway to the cell block.

Overcome with a sense of foreboding and trepidation, she almost agreed. It would be so easy to rely on his strength, to accept his protection. Then she thought better of it. She squared her shoulders and shook her head.

"No," she said. "It would only outrage him."

"So what?" Justin retorted with a touch of defiance. "Let him be outraged. Let him take a swing at me and give us one more thing to charge him with."

"No," she repeated, certain now that this was a confrontation she had to face alone. "I'll be safe enough."

Despite her claim, though, she was grateful that the cell door between them would be locked. Today's scene had proved her worst fears about Will's temper.

After taking one last look at Justin, she drew in a deep breath and went to see her husband, all the while trying to remember that this was a man she had once loved with all her heart.

Since she'd seen him being led away from Dolan's, all of the fight had drained out of him. He was sitting on the cot in his cell looking dazed, as if he weren't quite sure how he'd gotten there. He looked surprisingly chastened.

In the months since she'd last seen him, he'd aged. There were even premature hints of gray in his straight, coal black hair. There were shadows under his eyes and lines of weariness etched on his face. And yet, despite the obvious exhaustion, he was as handsome as ever, his clothes perfectly tailored, if badly mussed from his rampage at Dolan's. He would hate it when he realized how filthy and wrinkled he was.

"Will," she said softly.

His head jerked up and for a brief instant she saw the hint of vulnerability, the flash of a boyish smile that had made her fall in love with him when they'd first met. Then, as if he suddenly remembered the circumstances, his expression hardened and the light in his eyes died.

"You'll pay for this, Patsy," he said coldly.

"No," she said, refusing to cower under the threat. "You brought this on yourself. I wasn't the one smashing things up at Dolan's."

"If you'd opened the damn door…"

"You were out of control," she reminded him patiently.

"Because of you. You took my son. You ran away from our marriage and you did it when it would hurt me the most, right in the middle of a campaign. You deliberately humiliated me."

"You're wrong," she said, and met his gaze evenly. "I wasn't even thinking of you."

"There, you see. It didn't matter a damn to you that your leaving could cost me the election."

"No, it didn't. I was only thinking about saving myself and Billy."

He gazed at her incredulously. "From me?"

"Yes, from you. You'd turned our house into a war zone. I left you once because of it, but rather than change, you just threatened me and my parents. You virtually blackmailed me into coming back. This time I just made sure there was nobody else involved and I came to a place I prayed you'd never find me. Obviously it wasn't far enough."

His expression turned triumphant. "You should have known better than that. I have the resources to find you no matter where you try to hide. It would be wise of you to remember that if you ever get a crazy idea about leaving again.''

Patsy wrapped her arms around her middle and forced herself not to show how terrified she was that he might try to make her go home with him again.

''I'm not coming back to Oklahoma, Will, and neither is Billy.'' She said it firmly, her gaze fixed on his face as she waited for the explosion of temper likely to follow. To her amazement—and fear—there was no explosion, just a cold, cruel look.

''I guess we'll see about that,'' he said in a soft, lethal tone. ''Have you noticed that this cell has a window? It has a perfectly fascinating view of Main Street. I saw you and your boyfriend.''

Patsy barely contained a gasp of dismay. Surely he wouldn't drag Justin into the middle of their fight. She stared into his unrelenting eyes and sighed. Of course, he would.

''He is not my boyfriend,'' she said, hoping to persuade him.

''Oh, I'm sure I can find folks who'd say otherwise.''

''Pay them to, you mean.''

''If necessary.''

''It won't hold up, Will.''

''Are you willing to risk that? Is he worth losing Billy?''

Fury outdistanced fear. ''You will never take my son. *Never!*''

''Try me.''

"You won't win."

"Oh, but I will. I have money and power and influential friends. I can give Billy everything. He's half Native American. That'll work in my favor, too. Living with you would rob him of his heritage, keep him from understanding his father's culture. Tribal law—"

She cut him off. "Since when are you so concerned with your culture?" she snapped. "The only time it's mattered to you is when it can be exploited for your own political gain. Beyond that, you've turned your back on your people. When was the last time you spent even five minutes with your parents on the reservation? When did you ever give a damn about the customs of your people?"

As soon as the words were out of her mouth, she knew she'd made a mistake. She had touched a raw nerve. In fact, she suspected that most of her own problems with her husband arose from the fact that he knew in his heart that marrying her had been a betrayal of his roots, the final slap in the face of his family. He'd been proud of winning her love, only to resent the fact that he'd needed her by his side to become a more acceptable candidate for office.

"Then the best way to make amends will be to insure that my son is raised by his Native American family," he retorted. "It will happen, Patsy. Count on it."

"Will," she began, ready to beg. Then she caught herself. That was what he wanted. He wanted to see the fear in her eyes, wanted to hear it in her voice.

She wouldn't give him the satisfaction, even though she was quaking inside. Instead, she said quietly, "I'm sorry it's come to this. I really am. There was a time when I truly loved and respected you."

For a moment he seemed taken aback, but Patsy didn't wait to see what he might say next. She had to get away from him before she made things worse than she already had. Head held high, she walked out of the cell block. Only when she was back in the lobby with the door firmly closed behind her did she sag against it. Justin was there at once, concern written on his face as he led her to a seat beside his desk.

"What can I get you? Want some coffee? It's foul, but the caffeine might jolt some color back into your cheeks."

"No, thanks."

"What happened in there? What did he say to you?"

"The same old thing," she said wearily. "He's going to take Billy from me."

"Over my dead body," Justin said fiercely. "That is the one thing that will never happen."

"You can't guarantee that."

"Okay, maybe I can't," he conceded, "but Janet can." He tucked a hand under her elbow and hauled her to her feet. "Come on."

All Patsy wanted to do was go home and hold her baby, then crawl under the covers and hide for a month. But that was what the old Patsy would have done. She was stronger now. She had to keep reminding herself of that.

"Where are we going?" she asked as Justin half dragged her from the station.

"To see Janet. I've already called. She'll meet us at her office."

"I thought she'd retired."

"There's retired and then there's Janet's version of retired. She's giving it lip service for Grandpa Harlan's sake, but, believe me, she can't wait to find a case she can get her teeth into."

He grinned. "That's why she never quite got around to putting her office on the market, much less moving out her desk and files and law books. Personally, I think she sneaks into town and hides out there after telling Grandpa Harlan she's gone shopping, but I can't prove it. I've never caught her there. Then, again, I've never seen her carrying a lot of packages to her car, either."

"I don't want to be responsible for the two of them fussing with each other," Patsy said, still reluctant.

"Oh, Grandpa may bluster some, but he knows deep down that Janet loves being a lawyer too much ever to walk away from it entirely. At least he's gotten her to slow down, and he thoroughly enjoys letting her think she's putting something over on him."

Patsy sighed enviously. "They have a wonderful marriage, don't they?"

"The best. It's set a great example for the rest of us. As I understand it, my grandmother Mary adored my grandfather. She was the epitome of the traditional wife. She devoted herself to him, almost to the exclusion of their sons. When she died in a riding accident, Grandpa was devastated.''

He chuckled. ''Then, thanks to Jenny stealing his car, he met Janet.''

Patsy stared at him, flabbergasted. ''Jenny stole his car?''

''Oh, yeah. She was fourteen at the time. She crashed it into a tree.''

''I'll bet that got his relationship with her mother off to a rocky start.''

''You could say that. Janet was definitely not the kind of woman Grandpa was used to. For one thing she didn't bow to his every whim. I was pretty little when they met, but the stories are legendary about their courtship. Best of all, the sparks are still there. You can feel it whenever they're in the same room.''

He met her gaze. ''Just like us,'' he added softly.

Patsy had always wanted to believe that a relationship like that was possible. Her own parents had been married for years, but it was as much habit as love that kept them together. There was none of the warmth and tenderness she had witnessed between Janet and Harlan Adams. Theirs was the kind of relationship she'd always dreamed of, the kind she could almost imagine having with Justin if things were different. Maybe someday, though, as soon as this mess was straightened out once and for all.

They reached Janet's office and paused on the sidewalk out front.

''You ready?'' Justin asked, tucking a finger under her chin to tilt her face up so he could study it.

Thinking of Will's view of the street, she backed away, ignoring the flash of hurt in Justin's eyes. "I don't have any choice, do I?"

"Not unless you're willing to go back to Oklahoma with him and go through the same thing all over again."

"Never," she said adamantly.

"Then let's do it." He held open the door.

Inside, Janet rose to greet them. She gave Justin a kiss on the cheek, then enfolded Patsy in a hug.

"Justin's filled me in on the basics. It's going to be okay," she promised, her expression radiating a quiet serenity.

And for the first time in months, Patsy actually felt as if it might be.

Before Patsy realized what was happening, Janet was ushering a protesting Justin out the door.

"He can stay," she said, responding to the indignation on his face.

"No," Janet countered. "It will be best if we have this conversation in private."

"But—" Justin began, only to be cut off again.

"Go," Janet said. "You've done your part by bringing her here. Now, go away and have a cup of coffee or something."

Justin's gaze sought Patsy's. "You're okay with this?"

Patsy nodded. "Thanks to you, I'm in good hands."

"Well, of course. That's not the issue."

Janet smiled tolerantly. "Justin, go," she commanded softly.

He bent and brushed a kiss across Patsy's forehead. "I'll be at the office if you need me."

After he'd gone, Janet turned a thoughtful look on Patsy. "He's very protective of you, isn't he?"

"That's just his nature. It's probably why he became a cop."

"Sweetie, I don't think this has anything to do with his job. Whether he knows it or not, he's falling in love with you."

Patsy stared at her in shocked disbelief. "You're wrong. I mean, I know he cares about me and Billy, but love? No, it can't be."

"Why not? Because you don't love him?"

"I never said that."

Janet grinned. "Good, then we won't be starting out with any lies and half-truths between us."

Patsy studied her intently. "You tricked me, didn't you?"

"I suppose. I just wanted to be sure where things stood. I don't want Justin to be hurt. He has a tender heart." She shuffled some papers on her desk and got out a pen. "Now, tell me about you and Will Longhorn. From the beginning."

An hour later Patsy was still talking. She told Janet every single thing she could recall about their relationship, from the moment she'd gone to work in Will's office until she had run away and sought refuge for herself and her son in Los Piños.

Janet rarely interrupted and then only to ask very

pointed questions about something Patsy had said. When Patsy was finished, she regarded Janet evenly. "It's not a very pretty story, is it?"

"I've heard worse. How much of this does Justin know?"

"All of it." She hesitated, then said, "There is one more thing you should probably know. Will saw me with Justin earlier. He's threatened to drag him into it."

To her surprise, Janet chuckled.

"That will certainly make his day," she said. "He's already spoiling for a fight with this man. Heaven help Will Longhorn if he gives Justin an excuse."

"Justin can't be involved," Patsy said fiercely. "He's already paid a price for keeping silent rather than reporting me to the Oklahoma authorities. I know he struggled with his conscience every day over that."

"Justin knew you were wanted for kidnapping your son?" Janet asked, clearly surprised.

Patsy nodded. "It put him in a terrible position."

"Did you ask him to keep silent?"

"No, of course not. I didn't even realize how much he knew until yesterday. That's when he admitted that both he and Tate knew all about Will's claim. I guess Tate had buried the paperwork."

"Well, well, well," Janet murmured. "I've always known that Tate Owens was a good man, but to tell you the truth I've wondered when Justin would get the perspective he needs to do that job right."

Patsy was startled by the implied criticism. She rushed to Justin's defense. "Justin is an excellent lawman. You have to know that. He believes so fiercely in right and wrong."

"Exactly," Janet said. "Up until now it's been black-and-white with him. You're either obeying the law or you're breaking it, in spirit or in deed. Apparently he's finally discovered that there are some actual gray areas in life. It will make him a better policeman. Maybe he'll even find a way to forgive the man who hurt Sharon Lynn and killed Kyle."

"Has Sharon Lynn been able to do that?"

Janet looked deeply troubled by the question. "I'm not sure she ever thinks of him at all. She's still blaming herself."

"I was afraid of that. Do you think she needs to see a psychologist?"

"It doesn't matter what I think," Janet responded. "Sharon Lynn has to want to move on and right now she's too consumed with guilt to think about the future."

"Is she better physically?"

"She's getting stronger every day. She needs to start getting up and getting out."

Patsy gave that some thought. "I have an idea."

Janet's expression brightened. "Tell me."

"I know she'd been thinking about buying Dolan's. What if she were to think that Doc was about to leave and the rest of us were going to be out of jobs. She loves that place. Would she be able to bear the thought of it closing down?"

Janet pondered the idea, then nodded slowly. "It just might work. Particularly if you were the one to tell her, maybe lay it on really thick about how important the job is to you, especially now with the custody fight and your very expensive lawyer." She added the last with a grin.

"How expensive?" Patsy asked. "Are you really going to help me? Do we have a case?"

"Don't worry about my fee. We'll work something out. I'm grateful to have a case that my husband can't possibly disapprove of my taking. As for winning it, there's something you need to understand about me. I have never accepted losing as a possibility. That doesn't mean I haven't lost a time or two, but I always fight to win."

"But the system—"

"The system requires a fair fight. With all due modesty, with me on your side, the fight will be more than fair. I know how to handle the Will Longhorns of the world." She met Patsy's gaze evenly. "Tell me this, what are you most afraid of?"

"That Will will try to take the baby, insist on him being raised by the tribe. Isn't that what's happening with babies who are part Native American?"

"They won't take the baby from its natural mother. I promise. And given what you've told me about your husband, I doubt he'll fight the divorce or even whatever custody arrangements we want, not if he wants to run for political office," she said grimly. "He won't want all the details of his abuse made public."

"But—"

"No buts. Even if he tries to claim that the charges are false, he'll never be able to wash away all the mud on his reputation," Janet said with confidence. "If he's smart and his advisers truly believe in him, they'll convince him to settle this quietly and with as little publicity as possible. From everything you've said about him, I doubt Will Longhorn will be vindictive enough to throw away everything he's ever wanted just to get even with you."

For the first time since she'd fled, Patsy began to hope that she could finally stop running. Relief coursed through her. "Will I have to go back to Oklahoma?"

"No. We'll file the divorce papers right here. I'll have him served before he even gets out of jail." She came around the side of her desk and clasped Patsy's icy hands. "You and Billy will be fine, and you *will* be together. Trust me."

"He'll be furious when he gets the papers." She thought of his temper. "What if he comes to the house?"

"I'll ask for a restraining order."

Relieved, Patsy was ready to grasp at the option and then she thought of Billy. He wanted so badly to see his daddy. Could she keep them apart? Or did she owe it to Billy to let him maintain some sort of relationship with his father, however carefully guarded?

Finally she voiced her concerns out loud. "Billy's been asking to see his father. With Will right here, what should I do?"

Janet considered the question for some time. "We

can work it out, if it's what you want. It might be for the best, prove how reasonable we intend to be.''

''Not alone, though,'' Patsy said hurriedly. ''I don't want Will alone with him. He might take him and run.''

''A supervised visit, then. I think I know of a sheriff's deputy who'd be happy to hang out with the two of them or all three of you, if that's what you'd prefer.''

''Yes,'' Patsy said at once, thinking of the likely need for a buffer between the two men. Will was going to resent Justin's right to be there, and Justin was clearly itching for an excuse to slug him. ''I'd better be there.''

''Then when Will's released, we'll arrange for him to come to the house to see his son.''

''Thank you,'' Patsy said. ''For everything.''

''No need. I'm doing this as much for Justin as I am for you. You're good for him.''

''I've brought him nothing but trouble.''

''No,'' Janet corrected. ''You've opened up his heart.''

Chapter Twelve

When Patsy emerged from Janet's office into the bright sunlight, she couldn't help comparing it to emerging from the darkness of the nightmare Will had put her through these past few years. At last, though, the future was bright again. The debt she owed to the Adamses was enormous, beginning way back with Sharon Lynn.

Instead of heading directly to Justin's office, she went to Dolan's and found the elderly pharmacist filling prescriptions as methodically as ever, evidently unconcerned about the mess in the front of the store.

"Doc, I'm truly sorry about all of this. I'll pay for fixing it."

He peered at her over his reading glasses. "You didn't do it, did you?"

"Well, no, but—"

"Then I'm not laying the blame on you. It'll get fixed up. The glass cutter's already been here. Justin saw to it."

"But I should be the one—"

He grinned. "You're wasting your time arguing with me, young lady. If you disagree with the plan, you'll have to talk to Justin."

Patsy sighed. He was doing it again. He was fixing things for her. On the one hand, she was grateful. On the other, it was a reminder of too many years of weakness and dependence on other people.

"I'll speak to him," she said grimly.

The older man grinned. "Let me know how it turns out. It's been my experience that once an Adams makes up his mind, there's not much use in fighting him."

"We'll just see about that," Patsy retorted. "Before I go to see Justin, there's something else I want to discuss with you." She explained her idea for lighting a fire under Sharon Lynn and hopefully jolting her out of her depression. She didn't mention that the plot was helping her to keep her own mind off whatever was going on with Will down at the sheriff's office.

"Are you sure you're not an Adams?" he asked when she'd finished. "You're sneaky just like they are."

"You disapprove?"

"No, indeed. Not if it'll get the job done. I'll go along with anything that'll get that pretty little gal out of her bed and back among the living. I've just been putting off my retirement until she made up her mind whether she wanted to take this place off my hands.''

Impulsively Patsy hugged him. ''Thank you. Since the lunch counter's already covered, I'm going out to White Pines now, if you don't mind.''

''Go. Be sure to let me know how it turns out.''

''If I go about this right, you won't need me to tell you. Sharon Lynn will be busting down the door before the afternoon's over with.''

''Lordy, I hope not,'' he said with mock horror. ''One busted door in a day is about all an old man can cope with.''

''You know perfectly well what I mean.''

''Yes, I do. Now, get along with you.''

When she arrived at the ranch, she went straight up to Sharon Lynn's room in the main house. She found her friend still in bed, still gazing blankly at the ceiling.

''Hey, sweetie, how're you feeling?'' she asked, pulling a chair up beside the bed.

Sharon Lynn cast a distracted look her way, then gazed off in the distance again.

''I have some news,'' she said, deliberately injecting a somber note into her voice.

The statement drew no response.

''It's about Dolan's.''

There was a flicker of interest in Sharon Lynn's eyes, but nothing more.

''The Doc told me today that he intends to close it down.''

Sharon Lynn blinked rapidly at that, then turned slowly to face Patsy. "He's closing it?"

"Well, you know he's been thinking of retiring for some time. You told me that yourself. I guess he's decided it's time."

Sharon Lynn frowned. "But he knew I was thinking about buying it."

"I guess he figured since the accident and all, you wouldn't be interested, and he didn't want to wait around until another buyer showed up. I guess he's anxious to move on down to the Gulf Coast and go fishing."

The news clearly agitated her friend. Sharon Lynn began to fiddle with the pretty flowered comforter that was drawn up to her chin.

"This couldn't have come at a worse time," Patsy said sorrowfully.

"What do you mean?"

"I guess you haven't heard. My husband, Will, he showed up in town today and bashed down the door at Dolan's." Her shudder at the memory was only slightly exaggerated for Sharon Lynn's benefit. "Maybe that was the final straw for Doc. I don't know. Anyway, Will's in jail, and Janet's about to file divorce and custody papers. It's going to be expensive, and I'm out of a job again."

"You don't need to worry about that. Janet won't take your money anyway."

"Of course she will. I'm not accepting charity. It's important to me to prove I can stand on my own two feet. I'm sure you can understand that. Dolan's has always represented a certain amount of independence to you, too, hasn't it?''

"Yes, I suppose it has. I've never thought about it that way before. I just knew I liked working there. It gave me my own identity away from the family's ranching. Plus I was following in my mother's footsteps. She and Daddy did most of their courting in that place while she ran the lunch counter.''

"There, you see?'' Patsy said brightly. "I knew you'd understand.'' Then she sighed heavily. "Of course, I can probably find another job in another town.''

Sharon Lynn appeared genuinely shocked by the suggestion. "And leave Justin? You would do that to him?''

"Well, I wouldn't want to, but—''

The next thing she knew, Sharon Lynn had tossed off the comforter and was climbing out of bed. She brushed past Patsy.

"Oh, for heaven's sake, get out of my way.''

Patsy barely contained a hoot of triumph. "Why? Where are you going? Should you be out of bed?''

"I should have been out of bed days ago. As for where I'm going, you know perfectly well, I'm going to have a talk with Doc Dolan. I will not let Dolan's be closed down, and if anybody's going to buy that place, it's going to be me.''

Patsy regarded her innocently. "If you're sure…''

"I'm sure.''

Patsy kept up a steady barrage of doubts all the way to the front door, right past a gaping Harlan Adams. After they'd waltzed past him, Patsy turned around and caught his wink. Obviously Janet had filled him in on the plan, though he was clearly stunned to see it had worked.

"I really don't know if you should be going all the way into town your first day out of bed," Patsy said, along with half a dozen other protests designed to keep Sharon Lynn just irritated enough not to back down.

"Oh, will you just shut up," Sharon Lynn finally snapped. "I'm going and that's final."

"If you say so."

"Well, I do."

Outside, though, Sharon Lynn came to an abrupt halt. Patsy regarded her worriedly. "What is it? Is something wrong? Are you feeling faint?"

"I don't have a car," she whispered, her voice cracking. "And even if I did, I couldn't...I don't think I can ever drive again."

Patsy reached for her hand and squeezed. "Then isn't it a good thing that my car is here? I'll drive you into town, if that's what you want."

For a moment, Sharon Lynn looked as if she might back down, but then she squared her shoulders. "Perfect. I'm sure Justin or someone in the family will be coming out this way later. I can hitch a ride home with them."

"Or I'll bring you back. It's not a problem."

"Whatever." She walked over to Patsy's car and reached for the handle of the passenger door, then faltered. She swallowed hard. "I'm not sure..."

Patsy sensed that Sharon Lynn had to do this today or she might never try again. "You'll be fine. I'll drive very carefully."

"Of course you will. It's not that."

"Let me ask you something. Have you ever fallen off a horse?"

Sharon Lynn regarded her impatiently. "I grew up on a ranch. What do you think?"

"And what did your dad or grandfather tell you?"

"To get up and get back on."

"Same thing after an accident," Patsy said lightly, praying that she was giving the right advice.

"I'll never get behind the wheel of a car again," Sharon Lynn said fiercely, her expression anguished.

"You don't have to drive, if you don't want to, but you're bound to want to go places. How will you get into town every day, if someone doesn't bring you?"

"I'll move to town."

"Then how will you get back out here for family dinners and holidays?" Patsy asked reasonably.

"Oh, for heaven's sake," Sharon Lynn finally grumbled, and opened the door. "Let's just go and get it over with."

She maintained a white-knuckled grip on the edge of the seat all the way into town, but she didn't utter another protest. Still there was no question she was relieved when Patsy parked in front of the drugstore. She rushed out of the car as if she'd just been advised there was a bomb under the hood.

Thankfully, the glass cutter had been busy while Patsy had been at the ranch. Though the window displays hadn't been redone, at least there were shiny new windows in place. Sharon Lynn viewed the residue of the disaster with lifted brows, then walked inside. Heads turned as she sailed past the lunch counter and straight to Doc Dolan's place behind the prescription counter.

"We need to talk," she said in a no-nonsense tone.

"As soon as I finish getting Mrs. Phelps's pills ready for her," the pharmacist said without looking up.

"Now!" Sharon Lynn said fiercely.

"Sounds like she's back to her old self," Justin observed, coming up behind Patsy.

"Not yet, but I think she's getting there."

He rested his hands on her shoulders and turned her to face him. "You're a good friend, maybe even a bit of a miracle worker."

"There were no miracles involved. I just thought of a reason for her to get out of that bed. Thank God, it was the right one." Satisfied that everything had been set into motion at the back of the store, she met Justin's gaze. "Anything happen at the jail I should know about?"

"Your husband got the divorce papers."

Stunned by the speed with which Janet had worked, she asked, "Is the building still standing?"

"It was when I left. He's demanding a conference with Janet."

"Oh, dear."

"Not to worry. Janet was sitting in Tate's office waiting. She'd anticipated the request. She looked downright eager to have a little face-to-face with him."

"Did she tell you about the visitation with Billy?"

"I'll be there," he said softly. "Don't worry about it."

She regarded him worriedly. "You won't be looking for an excuse to shoot him, will you?" she asked, only partially in jest.

He grinned. "Not as long as he keeps his temper in check and Billy's glad to see him."

"Any idea when he'll be free to come over?"

He nodded. "That's why I came looking for you. He's going to be released right after his meeting with Janet. I thought you might want to go home to prepare Billy."

Patsy's knees turned weak at the prospect. She hadn't expected it to happen so soon, not on a day that had already been a roller coaster of emotional ups and downs. "Tonight?"

"Yes. Then with any luck he'll leave town. That's the deal for his release. Doc Dolan won't press charges if Will heads back to Oklahoma and never sets foot in Los Piños again except for liberal court-approved visits with his son." He stroked a finger down her cheek. "It's going to be over, Patsy. By this time tomorrow, it's finally going to be over."

She wanted to believe that, but she couldn't. Not yet. Not until she saw Will actually get in his car and drive away. Maybe not even then. Maybe not until he'd been gone for weeks or months and there'd been no attempts at payback.

The first step to insuring that Will would stick to their bargain and leave was to let him see Billy tonight. Needing Justin's strength, she reached for his hand and said in an unsteady voice, "Let's go home."

"I'll walk you over, then head back to the station," Justin said. "I'm going to escort him officially to your place after his release. After that, he'll stay overnight at a motel, then if all the details are ironed out in the morning and all the papers are signed to Janet's satisfaction, you can say goodbye once and for all."

If only it would go that smoothly, Patsy thought wistfully, but this was Will they were talking about. He didn't give up anything he considered to be his that easily.

Justin stood idly by as Will Longhorn signed himself out of jail. Tate made it a point to remind the lawyer of his agreement to be gone by the next day. For a brief instant, the man's arrogance threatened to erupt, but he finally set his jaw and nodded.

"If you're ready, I'll take you by Patsy's," Justin said when the last paper was signed.

"I can get there on my own," Will said, dismissing him.

Justin stood his ground. "Afraid not."

"More rules?" Will demanded sarcastically, but he followed Justin to the waiting patrol car. "What kind of town is this? Do you all just make up these regulations as you go along? Or are you taking particular pleasure in tormenting me?"

"We believe in the kind of justice it takes to get the job done," Justin said evenly as he drove the few blocks to Patsy's and pulled up to the curb in front. "If it requires a little creativity, so much the better."

Will glared at him. "Believe me, I know exactly what your agenda is. You think you're so smart, don't you? You think you've won."

"Where you're concerned, I don't have to win. This is all about your wife and son and what's right for them. If you've got a shred of decency in you, you'll set them free."

"It's not up to you."

Justin feared prolonging the debate would only make the other man's hackles rise. He was clearly spoiling for a fight and Justin was a handy target. If Justin thought about accommodating him, it might be enough to cause him to back out on whatever deal he'd agreed to with Janet. To prevent that from happening Justin remained tight-lipped.

"Nothing to say to that?" Will taunted.

"Maybe you should stop worrying about me and concentrate on your boy," Justin said mildly, gesturing toward the window where Billy was watching for them.

Even as they looked, Billy scrambled down and raced out the front door.

"Daddy, Daddy," he shouted as he toddled unsteadily down the walk.

To Justin's surprise, Will Longhorn bolted from the car, knelt down on the sidewalk and scooped his son into his arms. There were tears in his eyes as Billy's arms locked around his neck.

"I missed you, Daddy. I missed you lots."

"I missed you more," Will murmured, his voice thick with tears.

Justin felt his throat squeeze tight as he watched the two of them. The sight had shaken him more than he cared to admit. It was yet another reminder that not everything was as black-and-white as he'd always believed. His view of Will Longhorn had been colored by what he knew of the man's shabby treatment of Patsy. Now, seeing him with his son, he realized that whatever his faults, Will Longhorn loved his son and Billy returned that love. It wasn't a bond that could be broken lightly.

He glanced up and saw that Patsy was watching the scene with tears in her eyes. He went past the man and boy to stand beside her.

"How can I do it?" she wondered aloud. "How can I keep them apart? Billy still brings out the good in him."

"That's a heavy burden for a two-year-old. Will needs to find the good in himself some other way."

She sighed. "I know you're right, but—"

"No, darlin'. You're doing the right thing. I suspect if he's honest with himself, even Will sees that."

"I hope you're right," she said as Will stood up with Billy in his arms and started toward the house. Despite whatever trepidations she might be having, she managed a smile for them. Justin had never been prouder of her.

"Daddy's going to stay for dinner," Billy announced. "S'ghetti."

"That's right, munchkin. Your favorite."

Justin hid a smile. He'd seen the damage Billy could do to the surrounding area with a plate of spaghetti. He wondered how Will would feel when it wound up splashed all over his fancy clothes, even if they were a little the worse for wear.

He was in for a surprise on that score, too. Will never batted an eye when sauce splattered off Billy's exuberantly wielded fork. Patsy started out of her chair at the sight of the red stain, but Will waved her off.

"It's a suit," he said mildly. "It'll clean, or I'll get another one."

She stared at him in blatant amazement. Even Will grinned at her reaction.

"Okay, so I'm mellowing. Maybe I've finally started getting my priorities in order." He regarded her wearily. "Too bad it's too late, isn't it?"

"Yes," she said softly. "Yes, it is." And then she turned and gazed at Justin.

There was no mistaking the message in her eyes, and Will didn't pretend not to get it. He rose from the table and picked up his son. "I'll give Billy his bath and put him to bed, if you two don't mind. Then I'll be on my way."

"Fine," Patsy agreed, watching as he left the room and headed toward the bathroom with Billy pointing the way.

After he'd gone, she gazed at Justin. "He's changed."

With an odd, cold sensation in his chest, Justin stared at her evenly. "Enough?"

"No," she said, reaching out to lay a hand against his cheek. "It can never be enough."

Relief swept over him then. They weren't at the end of her troubles yet, but they were getting there. And when they did, Justin vowed that he would be waiting.

When it was time to escort Will to his motel, Patsy beckoned Justin back inside for a moment. He studied her expression, trying to guess what was on her mind.

"Second thoughts?"

"About Will and the divorce? No. I just wanted to ask you if you could come to dinner tomorrow night, alone, just the two of us?"

Justin's heart lurched and his blood began to pump a little faster. He had a thousand questions begging to be asked, but with Will waiting, there was no time. "Seven o'clock?" he asked.

She nodded. "That will be perfect."

"I'll be here."

Back outside he glanced at his watch and noted that it was already after nine. Less than twenty-two hours until he could return and by then Patsy Longhorn would be well on her way to becoming a free woman. He wondered if she could possibly be looking forward to that any more than he was.

Chapter Thirteen

Justin couldn't seem to make himself wait until dinnertime before catching a glimpse of Patsy. He strolled into Dolan's first thing in the morning and was stunned to find Sharon Lynn at work behind the counter. Even though he'd seen her talking to Doc Dolan the day before, he hadn't expected her to return full-time anytime soon.

"Hey, sweetheart, what are you doing here?"

She gave him a wry look. "I work here, or had you forgotten?"

Her tone suggested she didn't want to get into anything connected to her absence. Justin followed her lead. "Seems to me I do recall seeing you here a time or two. You cook a mean hamburger."

"I'm glad you approve, because I just bought the place."

Justin stared. This was a wrinkle he hadn't really anticipated. He knew she'd been toying with the idea, but to actually do it, especially considering her recent state of mind. He prayed she hadn't been pushed into making a hasty decision she would come to regret.

"You bought it?" he repeated slowly.

"Yesterday. Doc will stick around for a few more months until he's sure I understand how his part runs and until I find a replacement pharmacist, but it's all mine as soon as the bank works out the financing."

"Are you sure you're ready to take this on?"

She met his gaze evenly and her chin jutted stubbornly in typical Adams style. "I need it, Justin. Now more than ever. I couldn't lose it, too. Not after..." Her voice trailed off.

"Not after Kyle?" he asked gently.

She shook her head, blinking back tears. "He was my..."

"I know, sweetheart. Kyle was your world." He went around behind the counter and hugged her fiercely. "Do you know how proud I am of you?"

"Me? I haven't done anything."

"Sure you have. You've taken the first step toward getting on with your life. That's the hardest one. I guess for a minute there I was just surprised you'd taken such a big one."

"You can thank Patsy for that. She's a very clever woman."

He grinned. "I've noticed."

Sharon Lynn snagged a handkerchief from his pocket, brushed away tears and gave him a penetrating look. "Speaking of Patsy, I hear I'm not the only one who's getting on with her life."

"I have no idea what you're talking about," he claimed innocently.

"Yeah, right."

"By the way, where is she this morning?"

Sharon Lynn shot him a look of triumph that could have rivaled one of Grandpa Harlan's. "So much for the innocent act. And here I thought you'd stopped by just to visit with me."

"Just tell me where she is."

"Meeting with Janet and Will." She surveyed him knowingly. "Then she's taking the rest of the day off to get ready for her big date."

"Oh, you've heard about that, too, have you? The grapevine must be in really top form these days."

"No need to worry about that. She just discussed it with me to arrange for the time off."

"And you haven't been burning up the phone lines out to White Pines?"

"Not a peep," she swore.

"I would be eternally grateful if that remained true," he said.

She feigned disappointment. "For how long?"

"How about the next year?" He grinned at her shock. "Okay, at least until tomorrow."

Sharon Lynn nodded. "I can do that."

Justin slid onto a stool. "Now what does a guy have to do to get a cup of coffee around here?"

"Begging would be a good start."

"How about if I ask nicely and leave a big tip?"

"That would work, too."

Patsy was a nervous wreck. In a few minutes she was going to walk into Janet's office and the details of her divorce agreement with Will were going to be finalized. It would be over. Oh, there would be a wait for the final decree, but with Will not contesting, she would be free to move on with her life. Once the wheels had been set into motion, it had all happened so quickly her head was spinning. She could thank Justin and Janet Adams for that.

Janet claimed that dueling wits with Will Longhorn had been sheer pleasure and that no thanks were necessary, but Patsy intended to offer a more personal sort of thanks to Justin that night. She was going to show him how very grateful she was for everything he had done for her, from giving her a break on her first day in town, to arranging for Janet to intercede with Will.

In the meantime, though, there was one more thing she had to do. She had to talk to Will and try one last time to understand where everything in their marriage had gone so wrong. How much of it had been her fault? For too long she'd been willing to shoulder most of the blame, but she knew better now. Will was the one who'd changed and made their lives into a hell.

On the sidewalk outside of Janet's office, she drew in a deep breath, then turned the doorknob and walked in. She crossed the empty reception area and rapped on the office door even though it was wide-open. Janet and Will looked up at her knock.

"Good, there you are," Janet said, giving her a reassuring smile and beckoning her inside. "We were just going over the last little details."

"Everything's okay, isn't it?" she asked, the question directed at Janet but her gaze on Will.

He gave her a rueful smile. "I suppose that depends on your point of view, but in general everything is just fine. I'm not fighting you on anything. You've been generous with the visitation schedule, probably more generous than I deserve."

"Thank you for not fighting me."

"Don't thank me. I figure I owe you, and your lawyer has seen to it that I remember that."

"I don't want your money, Will." She turned to Janet. "I thought I made that clear."

"We've only asked for child support," Janet reassured her. "Billy deserves that."

"And I insist on it," Will said, his expression defiant.

"Yes, you're right," she said, backing down. "Of course there should be money for Billy. I can put it into a college fund."

Janet slid the papers across her desk. "Then let's get the last of these signed and everything will be official. I can file it with the court this afternoon."

Will cast one last look at Patsy, then turned back and signed the papers. Patsy followed with her own signature wherever Janet indicated.

"That's that, then," Janet said. She glanced at Patsy. "Would you two like a little time alone?"

Patsy nodded. "Please."

"I'll be in the next room, if you need me for anything."

After she'd gone, Will said, "An amazing woman, isn't she?"

"Yes, she is."

"I'd heard about her, of course, but the stories didn't do her justice. Seeing her in action reminded me of what being a good lawyer is all about." He met Patsy's gaze. "She's very protective of you, too. Is that because of Justin?"

"It's because she's a good lawyer, just as you said."

He shrugged. "I suppose."

"Can I ask you something, Will?"

"Why not?"

"What went wrong?"

He sighed heavily. "I wish I could begin to understand that. I certainly never meant to hurt you or Billy. I guess I didn't even realize how deeply words could cut or the kind of scars they could leave. I'm sorry."

There was a raw anguish in his expression that Patsy had never seen before. "Can you just explain why you seemed to hate me so? Was it because I'm not Native American?"

"Amazing," he said, clearly startled by the question. "I wonder if you hadn't figured that out long before I did. I began dating you, married you, for all the wrong reasons. You fit the image I thought I needed to go someplace. All those advisers I had around me concurred. They were ecstatic about our relationship. One day I just woke up and saw it as a betrayal of who I was. I blamed you for it, when the fault was my own.'' For the first time he looked directly into her eyes. ''Can you forgive me?''

Patsy thought of Justin, a man whose self-esteem was so strong, whose sense of family had never been tested. He would never struggle with who he was as Will had. And he was able to share his family and his strength with her. She'd never thought it possible, but she actually pitied Will for struggling to find a place in two sometimes incompatible worlds.

''Of course, I can forgive you,'' she said eventually. ''More important, though, can you forgive yourself?''

His smile was a mere ghost of the trademark Longhorn smile, the one that lit up his campaign posters and would no doubt seduce thousands of voters. ''I'm working on it.'' He moved closer and gently touched her cheek, his expression turning unbearably sad. ''See you around, Patsy.''

''Yeah. See you around.''

And then he was gone and in the blink of an eye she was on her own again. This time, she vowed, she was going to make sure she got it right.

Justin got through the rest of the day cruising on automatic. His mind certainly wasn't on work. It was fortunate for everyone that it was a quiet day. Everybody parked where they were supposed to and no one violated so much as the speed limit, much less any more serious laws. He spent most of the day catching up on paperwork.

"You still here?" Tate asked at six o'clock when he found Justin at his desk.

"Just killing a little time."

"Until your date with Patsy?"

"How the hell did you know about that?"

"My wife saw her picking up a couple of steaks at the supermarket. Plus she wasn't at work today and I saw Dani leaving the house a few minutes ago with Billy." He grinned. "Doesn't take a genius to add all that up, and I am a highly qualified sheriff. I make deductions a whole lot trickier than that all the time."

"You're also entirely too smug for your own good."

"So why aren't you at home getting ready?"

"How long can it take to shower and change?"

"What about stopping off to buy some flowers, maybe a box of candy? Women like those little touches. Trust me."

"When I want advice on my love life, I'll go to Grandpa Harlan. You may be a good cop, but he's a grand master at mapping out a courtship strategy. Of course, he rarely bothers with notifying the principals of his intentions where they're concerned. I'm just grateful he's left Patsy and me pretty much on our own."

"Once his wife mentions that those divorce papers got filed in court today, he might not be so reticent.

I'd suggest you take advantage of the time left to you before he starts meddling.''

Justin nodded. ''Good point. I'm out of here.'' He glanced at the clock and muttered a curse. It was after six.

Tate grinned and said innocently, ''By the way, I told Millie at the florist's you might be by for a bouquet of flowers. She's staying open till you get there.''

''Remind me to thank you one of these days.''

''Just make sure I get an invitation to the wedding.''

Justin was halfway down the block before Tate's words sank in. Who'd said anything about a wedding? Certainly not him. To be perfectly technical, this would be his very first date with Patsy. No one proposed on a first date, not when the ink wasn't even dry on the woman's divorce petition. Even with all the tricks at Janet's command it could be weeks or even months before the decree was final.

Still he couldn't seem to shake the idea once it had been planted. Wasn't that what the past few months had been leading up to? There wasn't a doubt in his head about how he felt about Patsy. Like all the Adams men, he might be a little slow at recognizing love when it was staring him in the face, but once he did, he couldn't see a whole lot of reasons for delaying the inevitable. Patsy, however, might not be quite so anxious to plunge into another marriage.

He was still reminding himself of that when he rang her doorbell promptly at seven, a huge bouquet of daffodils and bluebonnets in his hand. When she opened the door, she took his breath away.

She was wearing a pale yellow sundress that bared just enough of her shoulders and cleavage to make his mouth go dry. Her hair fell in waves to her shoulders, and moist color on her lips had turned her shy smile sexy. He swallowed hard.

"You look beautiful," he finally managed to say.

"So do you," she said, then blushed furiously. "I meant the flowers. They're lovely."

He shoved them into her hands, then cursed the fact that he suddenly felt like an awkward adolescent on his very first blind date ever, instead of an experienced man having dinner with an attractive woman he'd known for months.

"Dinner will be ready in a few minutes," she said, turning and leading the way through the dining room.

"Steaks," he said even before they reached the kitchen.

She glanced over her shoulder. "How did you know?"

He winced at the slip of the tongue. He absolutely refused to tell her that half the town probably knew. "I can smell the charcoal," he improvised. "Want me to throw them on the grill?"

"Would you mind? I'll finish up the salad."

Justin almost chuckled at her eagerness to get him out onto the patio and out of her way. It was clear she was every bit as nervous as he was. He found that as endearing as everything else about her.

He had the steaks on a plate and was about to come

back inside just as she came through the screen door.
They were standing toe to toe, gazes locked.

"I was just coming to check..."

"The steaks are done. I was just coming back in
to..."

She covered her face and turned away. "Oh, God,
I can't do this."

Justin stared at her, appalled. "Can't do what?"

"Nothing."

He brushed past her and set the platter of meat on
the kitchen table, then turned to draw her into his
arms.

"What's going on here?" he asked.

"I wanted everything to be perfect."

He was still confused. "It is perfect."

"No, it's not," she mumbled with a sniff. "I've
ruined it."

"How? We haven't even sat down at the table
yet."

"I don't mean the dinner."

Now he was more confused than ever. "What
then?"

She gazed up at him with tear-filled eyes. "Justin,
would you do something for me?"

"Anything."

"Kiss me, please."

He stared at her for no more than a heartbeat, before murmuring, "Now, darlin', that would be my
pleasure."

He lowered his head and brushed his lips across
hers, tasting the salty dampness of tears on her skin.

It was the first tentative hint of a kiss, no more, but it might as well have been the most passionate one he had ever shared. Heat and yearning and desire slammed through him. He wound his fingers through her silky hair and stilled her head beneath his as he continued to explore the exquisite texture and taste of her mouth.

She moaned softly and opened her mouth to his tongue. Her body molded itself to his, every curve fitting snugly against the hard planes of his body. The intimate contact sent images streaking through his mind of the two of them tangled together in his bed.

"We have to stop," he said on a ragged breath, pulling away.

"Why?"

"Because this is happening too fast. It's all wrong."

"It's not wrong," she insisted. "Not if we both want it."

Holding her at arm's length, gazing into her eyes, he admitted to himself for the first time without reservations that he had fallen deeply in love with this fragile yet brave woman. Whether she loved him, though, was another matter. What he saw in her eyes was nothing more than gratitude, mixed in perhaps with a whole lot of lust.

"Is this what tonight was about?" he asked gently. "Did you ask me over so you could seduce me?"

"You want me," she said. "I know you do."

"That's not the issue."

"What else is there?"

He smiled ruefully. "If you have to ask that, then we really are on the wrong wavelength."

"I want you to make love to me, Justin."

He heard the urgency in her voice, but it wasn't the urgency of desire. It was, he was sure, the need to settle a debt and it broke his heart.

"Not like this," he admonished her softly.

"Like what?"

"This isn't the way to say thanks, Patsy. Dinner will do for that just fine."

She started as if he'd slapped her. "You think I was offering myself to you out of gratitude?" she demanded.

"Weren't you?"

The question hung in the air, adding to the already high tension. Her expression faltered under his steady gaze.

"Okay, yes," she said finally. Eyes blazing she met his gaze. "But it was more than that. It is more than that."

"Tell me, then."

Her temper died slowly and only then did she murmur in a voice so low he could barely hear it, "I think I'm falling in love with you. It scares me to death, but there it is," she said with a defiant tilt to her chin.

Justin's heart flipped over. With some other woman maybes might have been enough. Not with this woman. With Patsy he wanted it all. He wanted love, commitment, permanence. He wanted a family and forever, with no doubts at all.

He bent his head and touched his lips to hers, then

headed for the door because he knew he didn't dare stay. He glanced back, saw her shattered expression and almost changed his mind, but something warned him that it would be the worst mistake of his life.

After taking one last look at this woman who'd stolen his heart, he sighed, then said, "Let me know when you're sure."

He almost made it out the door, but her softly whispered cry of his name stopped him. He turned slowly back.

"I know now," she said, her eyes bright.

He smiled. "So fast?"

She nodded. "Because you were willing to walk out of here when I know you didn't want to. I knew in that instant."

He wanted desperately to believe her.

She held out her hand. "Please stay. Just for dinner, if that's all you're interested in."

"You know better than that."

"Please stay," she repeated.

Still wondering if he could trust himself, he grinned. "No hanky-panky?"

"Absolutely not." She sketched an X across her heart, then regarded him innocently. "Unless you change your mind."

"The steaks are probably ruined," he noted.

"We probably shouldn't be eating meat, anyway."

"Don't ever say that out at White Pines," he warned. "Grandpa Harlan will surely take offense. He does run a cattle empire, you know."

"I'll remember that." She tilted her head. "So was that a yes? Are you going to stay?"

He considered the question for some time, debating the wisdom of his decision, weighing desire against reason. Finally he nodded.

"Against my better judgment."

She laughed at his somber tone. "What's the matter, Deputy? Don't you trust yourself around me?"

"You've got that right."

"I'll do my best to see that you don't go against any of those important principles of yours."

"There's only one principle that applies to this particular situation," he told her.

"What's that?"

"I don't want to do anything that either one of us is going to regret in the morning."

She stepped up close then, deliberately crowding him, and rested her hand against his cheek. His skin heated under her touch. "There is nothing we could do, Justin, *nothing,* that I would ever regret."

She said it so fiercely, with so much passion that Justin's only choice was to kiss her. He moved quickly, before he could think, before second thoughts could come roaring back. And when he claimed her lips this time, he knew there would be no turning back.

Until the very instant when Justin's mouth had come crushing down on hers again, Patsy had been terrified that he would walk out the door. She had also been very much afraid that she would never again have the courage to go after him. It had been a long time since she'd taken an emotional risk. Her confidence was shaky.

She had been astonished earlier when he'd read her so easily, when he'd guessed that she'd wanted to give herself to him out of gratitude. Men weren't supposed to be so perceptive. Then, again, this wasn't most men they were talking about. This was Justin. He'd always struck her as a cut above the rest and tonight he had proved it.

She wanted him so desperately. She wanted the physical connection, knowing that it would come with the emotional commitment. She had been so sure that she was doomed to a life of solitude, a life on the run, an unending marital limbo. Because of Justin, all that had changed. He had given her back her life, given her back her heart. So, yes, she was grateful.

She was also wildly, passionately in love with him. There wasn't a doubt in her mind about that now. She had told him the honest-to-God truth about that. She had known, though, that he was really asking more than that. He was asking not just about her feelings, but about her readiness to face the future, a future with him very much in the middle of it. Could she answer that question as easily? Truthfully, no. She'd made so many resolutions about standing on her own two feet. It was important to keep them.

But with Justin's mouth covering hers, with his hands dancing over her skin and setting off wildfires in the wake of his touches, the only answer she could give was with her body and she gave it eagerly.

Clothes were shed in a frenzy, his, hers, flying through the air and landing who knew where. His heated gaze was as seductive as his caresses, lingering on every inch of bared flesh, stirring her.

He slowly slid his hand along her belly toward the hook of her bra. He flicked it open, then slowly brushed away the scraps of lace. She watched the muscle in his jaw work as he stared at her breasts.

"You are so beautiful," he whispered for the second time that night, his breathing ragged. "I want to make love to you right here, right now."

"In the kitchen?" she said on a gasp that was as much pure pleasure as shock as he skimmed his finger across an already hardened nipple.

"You'll never prepare a meal in here again without remembering," he teased.

"I'm not sure my heart will be able to take it."

"Now, see, there's something I didn't know about you. You're very traditional."

Patsy glanced at the counter, then considered that they were both already mostly undressed. "I can change," she said thoughtfully. "It could be fascinating."

He chuckled. "You've turned daring now? In the blink of an eye?"

She felt laughter bubbling up. "It's been that kind of day."

"Come here then," he suggested, stealing away the last scraps of clothes she was wearing and hoisting her onto the counter. The tiles were cold, a startling contrast to the fire burning inside her.

When he lowered his head to take her breast in his mouth, she rocked back, stunned by the sheer magic of it. He shucked off his jeans and briefs, guided her legs around his waist and then he paused. Anticipation had her ready to plead with him, but then she saw that he was only reaching for a foil packet in his pocket.

And then, before the heat had cooled even so much as a degree, he was inside her and it was building again. So much heat, so much urgency. Patsy was trembling from the inside out, straining toward an elusive goal that promised release. She kept thinking about the magic of it, the wonder of being touched by a man who was totally, thoroughly dedicated to her pleasure.

And then she wasn't thinking at all, just feeling as Justin's thrusts went deeper, as tension coiled in her belly, then sent shock waves ricocheting wildly through her. The intensity of it shattered her, leaving her panting and sated and awed by the wonder that was Justin.

Chapter Fourteen

It was morning before Justin was finally able to force himself to leave Patsy's bed. They had finally made their way into it long after midnight. In the meantime, they had used Patsy's newfound daring to make love in several spots along the way.

Gazing at her with the morning sun splashed across her body, he was struck anew by what a remarkable woman she was. Definitely full of surprises, that was for sure.

He dressed quickly and paused beside the bed for one last, lingering look. She stirred as if she'd felt his gaze. She came awake slowly, stretching like a sinuous cat and setting his blood to roaring through his veins all over again. When her eyes finally focused on him, she blinked.

"You're already dressed."

"I need to get to work and I have to stop by the house first to change into my uniform."

She glanced at the clock. "Oh my gosh, I'm going to be late, too."

"Take your time. I've got an in with your boss."

She scowled. "Which you are not to use. Getting there on time is my responsibility. I'm supposed to open up. Sharon Lynn's not ready to be back full-time yet." She yawned.

"The impression I got is that she's anxious to be busy."

"I'm going in," she repeated emphatically.

Justin decided he'd better not argue with her. He'd seen evidence of this stubborn streak before, and after growing up with a whole clan of control freaks, he knew better than to take her on over the inconsequential stuff.

"Just don't burn the coffee."

"You can't burn coffee."

"You can if you forget to put any water in the pot. Ask Sharon Lynn. She has firsthand experience."

"When she was distracted by the wedding preparations?"

"Oh, yeah. And that was just the tip of the iceberg. Suffice it to say, you will always be regarded as something of a savior of the public health in this town."

She tilted her head. "Is that how you think of me?"

"No way, darlin'." He leaned down and whispered in her ear, chuckling when her cheeks turned bright red. "That's how I will think of you from now on."

"Well, I certainly hope you're the only one who feels *that* way."

"I'd better be," he concurred. He leaned down and delivered a hard, quick kiss that made up in intent what it lacked in passion. It was meant as a final reminder that she was his now. The dazed look in her eyes suggested he'd gotten his message across.

"See you in a while," he said.

"Justin, we are going to keep quiet about this, aren't we? For now, at least?"

He grinned, knowing the futility of it. "We can try."

She sighed. "I was afraid you were going to say that."

The whole blasted town was jumping to conclusions. Patsy realized it when half a dozen people asked very pointed questions that morning about her dinner with Justin and none of them had even witnessed the warm, personal greeting he gave her when he stopped by for a quick cup of coffee just before nine. Nor had most of them seen the way she'd brightened at his entrance. No, indeed, their probing had been sparked by something else entirely.

Thoroughly embarrassed at having her private life made public, she mumbled evasive answers to the prying questions and retreated to the back room at Dolan's every chance she got. Obviously Justin had known what he was talking about. There hadn't been a chance in hell of keeping anything secret in this town. It was all too reminiscent of being the wife of a promising political candidate.

"Hiding out again?" Sharon Lynn inquired, peeking through the partially opened door.

"I am not hiding out."

"Sure you are. Can't say I blame you. The folks in Los Piños do like their breakfast served up with gossip."

Patsy sighed. "What I can't figure out is how they even knew Justin and I were having dinner last night."

"That's a no-brainer."

"Explain."

"Did you shop at the grocery store?"

"Of course."

"Enough food for two, maybe something a little special, like thick steaks?"

She began to see where this was heading. "Yes."

"Did he bring you flowers?"

"Yes, but—"

"Did I cover for you in here yesterday afternoon?"

She got the picture. "Oh, good grief," she muttered impatiently. "Am I going to have to buy food in the next town before I invite him over again?"

Sharon Lynn grinned. "It won't help. We have sources there, too." She sat down on a stack of boxes. "So, tell me, how did it go?"

"We had a great time."

"Did you sleep with him?"

"Sharon Lynn!"

Her friend—and his cousin, she must never forget

that—grinned impudently. "Never mind. I think you've just answered that question."

"I did not."

"That bright pink color in your cheeks did."

"Maybe I was just embarrassed that you would even think such a thing."

"If you're trying to persuade me I'm wrong, it's not working. Justin couldn't look me in the eye and give me a straight answer, either."

"You asked him, too?"

"Well, of course I did. I love both of you. I want this to work out."

"Then maybe you should just leave us alone. Knowing there's a fascinated audience panting for a play-by-play won't help."

"If you think I'm nosy, wait until you run into Grandpa Harlan."

"Did I hear somebody mention my name?" the very man in question called out. "Where the dickens are you, girl? You hiding in the broom closet like your mama and Cody used to do?"

Patsy sent a panicked glance toward the door. "I am absolutely not going out there."

"Of course you are," Sharon Lynn said, clearly eager to throw her to the wolves—or one wolf in particular, at least. "Your break's over. Mine's just beginning."

Before Patsy could argue that point, the door pushed open and Harlan Adams poked his head in. He was evidently tired of waiting for either of them to appear.

"I knew it," he gloated. "What is it about this room that lures everybody back here?"

"Maybe they're hoping for a little privacy," Sharon Lynn teased, going over to give him a kiss on the cheek.

He seemed fascinated by the explanation. "You two indulging in a little girl talk? Mind if an old man sits in?" He glanced at Patsy. "I have a few questions about you and my grandson."

"Sorry, sir. You'll have to get those answers from Justin," Patsy said, slipping past him with the finesse and speed of a very crafty running back.

"Dadgumit, he wouldn't tell me a blasted thing, either," he grumbled irritably.

"Bless his heart," Patsy murmured.

"What was that?" Harlan Adams asked.

"She said he's a wise man, Grandpa. What she had the good grace not to say was that you're being a nosy old man."

He scowled at her. "Like you haven't been poking at her all morning long."

Sharon Lynn shrugged. "I'm her friend. I'm entitled."

His gaze narrowed. "Did she tell you anything?"

"No, I did not," Patsy said, giving Sharon Lynn a warning look. "Some people just enjoy making assumptions."

"How the devil is a man supposed to plan a wedding, if nobody will tell him anything."

Patsy halted in her tracks. A wedding? Who the

hell had said anything about a wedding? Sharon Lynn shot her a sympathetic albeit an I-told-you-so look.

"Maybe you should let the people involved make their own wedding plans, Grandpa, if there are any to be made."

He stared hard at Patsy. "That what you want?"

"I think it would be best," she agreed, then relented just a little at his look of disappointment. "I will tell you one thing, though. If and when Justin and I talk about getting married, you will be the first to know."

He gave a little nod of satisfaction. "Good enough." He bent down and kissed Sharon Lynn's cheek, then Patsy's. "I'd best be getting back to White Pines. Janet's been moping around out there this morning because she doesn't have a case to work on. I've got to come up with something to keep her occupied or she'll be back here in town practicing law full-time before I can blink. That case of yours sparked her hunger to work again."

Sharon Lynn winked at Patsy. "Maybe you should compromise, Grandpa. Let her take on a case now and then."

"She is a very good lawyer," Patsy offered. "It's a shame not to take advantage of all that legal knowledge."

"You two are just too danged liberated for your own good. Her place is home with me. It's taken me too darn long to get her there as it is."

"She'll be happier if she's feeling fulfilled professionally," Sharon Lynn said.

"Which means she will be very, very grateful to you for suggesting that she go back to work part-time," Patsy said slyly. She did not mention just what form that gratitude might take, even though she had some very recent experience with it.

He regarded Patsy with a twinkle in his eyes. "I do like the way you think, girl. I hope you and my grandson hurry up and get this show on the road."

"Why don't you forget about Justin and Patsy and pester Harlan Patrick," Sharon Lynn suggested. "Now there is a man just ripe for matrimony."

"Never you mind your brother. He's right on track with Laurie Jensen, as far as I can tell."

"And you would know, I'm sure," Sharon Lynn teased.

He scowled at her. "I have to see to it that all my babies are settled, don't I?"

"You think you do, anyway," she agreed.

Harlan Adams's expression sobered. "What about you, darlin' girl? You doing okay?"

The smile on Sharon Lynn's face faded faster than the sun dipping below the horizon. Patsy gave her hand a squeeze.

"She's doing fine," Patsy said, trying to bring a quick end to the subject. She was all too aware that Sharon Lynn's tears were too close to the surface and that the slightest reminder of Kyle could bring them coursing down her cheeks again. She'd dashed into this back room a few times herself today, when a customer's sincere expression of sympathy had gotten to be too much for her.

Thankfully, Harlan Adams glanced at Sharon Lynn and took Patsy's hint. He rose to his feet, again kissed his granddaughter on the cheek, then pressed another kiss on Patsy's cheek.

"I'll be getting on home now. As for you two, you might want to come out of this broom closet every now and again. It looks to me like there are some impatient folks sitting out here wondering what happened to the help."

"I'll go," Patsy said at once, brushing past him to discover that the only impatient person in the store was Justin. Her heartbeat accelerated. She forced herself to walk slowly back to the counter, pausing to grab a cup and the coffeepot on her way to where he sat.

"Back so soon?" she asked.

"Had to get my hourly fix of the prettiest woman in Los Piños," he teased.

"Sharon Lynn, get out here," Patsy called. "Justin's looking for you."

He grinned. "Very funny."

He looked past her just then and spotted his grandfather. To Patsy's amusement, he regarded him suspiciously.

"What are you doing here?" he asked.

"Do you think you're the only one in the world who appreciates a beautiful woman?" his grandfather asked.

"Go find your own. This one's mine," Justin said.

"Says who?" Patsy inquired.

"Whooee," his grandfather said, grinning. "I like this girl."

Justin turned his gaze from his grandfather to Patsy. His expression sobered. "So do I, Grandpa. So do I."

"Then I'll just run along and leave you to see what you can do about getting her to change her mind about you."

After he'd gone, Justin focused on Patsy. "So, what about it? Can I change your mind?"

"About?"

"Being mine."

Something in his tone told her the question wasn't being asked in jest. And as desperately as one part of her wanted to say yes, another part reminded her that once before she'd been too eager to jump into a relationship. She hadn't even fully extricated herself from that mistake yet.

"Maybe one of these days," she said. She glanced around to make sure they were unobserved, then leaned across the counter to brush a kiss across his lips. "You are awfully cute."

When she would have drawn away, Justin tucked his hand around the back of her neck and held her still long enough to deepen the kiss into something wild and sweet.

"Have dinner with me tonight," he suggested when he released her.

"Two nights running. People will talk," she teased.

"Darlin', I'm beginning to think it's our civic duty to give them something fascinating to talk about."

"That sounds a little too self-serving to me."

He grinned. "I was going for noble. What about it, though? Will you have dinner with me? We'll go someplace quiet and romantic."

Patsy had been to most of the restaurants in town. None she knew qualified. "Where?"

"You'll see."

"Justin, I really think you ought to tell me. I have a son to consider."

"Taken care of. He's going out to the ranch to spend the night. Janet says she can't wait."

Once again, he was taking over, smoothing things out to get his own way. Maybe under other circumstances she would have found the gesture touching. Instead, it rankled.

"Don't you think you should have consulted me before making arrangements for my son?" she asked testily.

"The plans aren't cast in stone," he replied, his tone reasonable. "If you have a problem with them, we'll change them."

"That's not the point."

"Then what is the point?" he asked patiently.

"I don't need somebody to run my life for me, Justin. I've been there, done that, and I didn't like it."

He nodded slowly. "I see."

"Do you really?"

"I think so. Will pretty much set the agenda for your lives and expected you to fall in line. How am I doing so far?"

There was that perception of his kicking in again to surprise her. "On the money," she admitted.

"I'll try to be more sensitive to that in the future," he promised.

She shrugged, not entirely trusting an easily made and easily broken promise. The proof would have to come over time.

He gave her one of his crooked, endearing smiles. "Can we start this conversation over again?"

She hesitated, then grinned back, unable to resist him in the end. "What the heck, give it a try."

"Patsy, would you care to have dinner with me tonight?"

"I'd be delighted," she said, because she could recognize the stupidity of turning down a date with a man she loved just to make a point.

"What about a baby-sitter for Billy? Need any help in making arrangements?"

"I'll volunteer," Sharon Lynn offered, joining them.

It was impossible to tell how much of the earlier conversation she'd overheard, but Patsy was grateful for the offer. "Are you sure you won't mind?"

"Heavens, no. It'll be fun. I can even stay over at your place. That way I won't have to have someone from the ranch come into town to pick me up tonight and you won't have to rush back home." She grinned. "In fact, you could stay out all night if you wanted to."

Patsy almost laughed at the hopeful expression on

Justin's face. "Okay, it's a deal," she said. "Thank you."

"No," Sharon Lynn said softly. "You're the one doing me a favor."

Her expression was so sad that Patsy was taken aback. She had seen firsthand how getting into a car had panicked Sharon Lynn. Now she realized just what a toll the trips into town and home again were taking. Suddenly she knew that if she weren't staying in Dani's old place, Sharon Lynn would have snatched it up for herself to rid herself of the frightening commute.

Before she could second-guess herself, she said casually, "You know, Sharon Lynn, if you wanted to, you could stay with Billy and me for a while."

The suggestion startled both Justin and Sharon Lynn, but Sharon Lynn seized on it with such a look of relief that Patsy knew she'd done the right thing.

"Are you sure you wouldn't mind? It would save me..." She hesitated, then sighed, not quite meeting Patsy's gaze. "It would save a lot of time."

Patsy met her gaze evenly. "I understand, and it would be fine with me. And I have no intention of thinking of you as a built-in baby-sitter. I'll enjoy the company."

"What about my company?" Justin demanded irritably.

"You, cousin dear, are an entirely different kind of company," Sharon Lynn teased. "And I'm sure she enjoys that, too."

"I do," Patsy assured him.

"Then we're on for dinner?"

"We are definitely on for dinner."

He grinned. "And after?"

"Don't push your luck, lawman. We'll negotiate the details over dinner."

He touched a finger to his Stetson in a mock salute as he put it back on. "I'll be looking forward to it, ma'am. What time shall I pick you up?"

"Why don't I pick you up?" she suggested, as a perfectly fascinating idea occurred to her.

"Why not? I'm a flexible kind of guy."

"That'll be the day," Sharon Lynn taunted.

He scowled at his cousin, then said to Patsy, "Don't listen to a thing she says about me. She's never forgiven me for laughing when she fell off a horse in front of…" The teasing light in his eyes died. "Oh, God, I'm sorry, sweetie."

Tears welled up in Sharon Lynn's eyes, but she reached over and touched Justin's lips. "Don't be sorry. Don't ever be sorry for reminding me of the good times. It's just that…"

"It's just that the wound is still raw," Justin said. "But you're going to be okay, you know that, don't you?"

"Sure," she said, forcing a wobbly smile. "We Adamses are made of tough stuff."

"The toughest," Justin concurred.

But looking at the tenderness in Justin's expression as he watched Sharon Lynn, Patsy knew he was wrong. Justin Adams, at least, had the softest heart she'd ever seen.

* * *

Justin had no idea why it had been so important to Patsy to pick him up that night, but he was going nuts waiting for her. Was this how women felt all the time waiting for their dates to arrive? No wonder some of them were itching to turn into control freaks.

Oh, he'd recognized what that whole discussion at Dolan's had been about that afternoon. Will Longhorn had dictated every aspect of his wife's life and she didn't intend to let it happen again. He had to wonder, though, how long these bids for independence were likely to go on. Would she refuse to marry him just to prove she could get along on her own? Or could he persuade her that it was possible to be half of a whole without losing her own identity? Tonight would be a fascinating test of his theory that she needed to know that at least some of the decisions in their relationship were hers to make.

When the doorbell rang at last, he bolted to answer it. To his astonishment, in spite of the humid evening air and clear skies, Patsy was wearing a raincoat.

"Expecting a storm?" he inquired lightly.

She gave him an enigmatic look. "In a manner of speaking. May I come in?"

He stepped aside. "Be my guest."

She sailed past him in a cloud of very seductive perfume. By the time he could recover from that and had closed the door, she had disappeared.

"Patsy?"

"Back here," she said in a tone that could have lured ships to crash into rocky cliffs.

There was no question that her voice was coming

from the bedroom, his bedroom, unless he missed his guess. He swallowed hard. Something told him that dinner was going to be very late and was going to consist of whatever was in his freezer.

When he got to the door to his room and glanced inside, his mouth gaped. Patsy was standing in the middle of the room in a black negligee so scanty he thought for sure his heart would slam to a stop if he stared at her too long.

"Won't you get cold at the restaurant?" he asked when he could find his voice.

Her confident expression faltered just a little. "You still want to go out?"

He barely held back a grin at her wistful tone. "Not if you don't."

"I thought I was making myself pretty clear."

"It wouldn't be the first time we've gotten our signals crossed."

"Justin, you will never make sheriff if you can't read a clue this obvious."

He grinned. "Okay, let me try." He paused thoughtfully. "You are less interested in dinner than you are in seduction."

She stepped toward him and nodded. "Very good," she praised.

She slid her arms around his neck. "And this?"

"No waiting?"

"Oh, yes," she murmured just before she stood on tiptoe and kissed him with an enthusiasm that left not a single doubt in either of their minds about how they were going to spend the rest of the evening.

Chapter Fifteen

Patsy was very proud of the way she'd managed to render Justin Adams totally speechless. Lying next to him in his bed, she felt as if she'd finally come home, finally met a man who thought of her as an equal, a partner. Maybe she was being a fool for setting some artificial time constraint on the relationship.

"Satisfied?" he asked, regarding her with an amused look.

"Oh, my, yes," she said.

"What happens now?" he asked.

Her expression faltered. "I guess that depends on you."

"Oh, no, you don't, Patsy Gresham Longhorn. For the past twenty-four hours you've been telling me every way you knew how that you are capable of making your own decisions, capable of taking the initiative, capable of standing on your own two feet, that you *insist* on standing on your own two feet, come what may.''

"There are still some things that are a man's prerogative,'' she admitted unwillingly.

"Such as?''

She was not going to put these words into his mouth. Nor was she quite brave enough to demand that he marry her and make an honest woman of her. Maybe if neither of them could put the question into words, there was a reason for it. Maybe it really was too soon after Will.

Even if she did absolutely adore being in his bed, with his arms around her and her head resting against his chest.

She sighed, rolled over and stood up. Justin regarded her with surprise.

"Where are you going?''

"You promised me dinner.''

"Sorry, darlin'. The cupboard's practically bare.'' He grinned. "We could order in. That would certainly make Angie's day over at the Italian restaurant. Or we could call Rosa and ask her to deliver some Mexican. Of course, she is related to the housekeeper at White Pines, which means there would be more talk.''

"Are you saying there is not one tiny little scrap of food in this house?''

"Not even a cracker.'' He surveyed her thoroughly.

"And you're not exactly dressed to go to the restaurant I had in mind." He beckoned to her. "Maybe if you climb back into bed I can make you forget all about your growling tummy."

"I'm sure you could," she agreed. "But without food neither of us will survive another round of really energetic sex."

"Then we'll take it nice and slow," he said in a provocative way that set her blood to pumping furiously.

She was still standing there debating the wisdom of that when Justin's beeper went off. In an instant, he was all cop. He grabbed the beeper from his nightstand, reaching for the phone at the same time.

"What is it?" he demanded, even as he scrambled to find clothes. His expression sobered. "I see. Okay, I'm on my way."

He slammed the phone down, pulled on his shirt and unlocked the drawer to get his gun. Patsy watched him and shivered. It was a full minute before he glanced her way and noticed her expression.

"I'm sorry," he said.

"No, it's okay. Of course, you have to go. What's happened?"

"We've got a high speed chase on the interstate heading this way. Tate wants me to set up a roadblock."

Patsy's blood ran cold as images of Sharon Lynn's wrecked car came whirling back.

He touched a finger to her cheek. "Don't worry. I know what I'm doing."

"I know. It's just that…"

"The accident," he said succinctly. "I'll be fine, Patsy. We have important things left to finish here tonight. I'll make sure I get back before you even miss me."

"Not possible," she told him softly. He wasn't out the door and she missed him already.

The instant he was gone, panic began to set in. What if he never came back? What if something happened and she'd never told him just how desperately she loved him? What if she'd wasted precious time while trying to declare her independence? Would it be worth it?

Maybe, she told herself as she sat huddled in a blanket on the sofa waiting for him, maybe when something was so clearly right, only a fool would take a chance on throwing it away.

When the clock ticked on slowly and still Justin hadn't returned, Patsy could no longer sit still. Despite his earlier claims that there was no food in the place, she went into the kitchen in search of something to eat.

When that proved fruitless, she went back to the bedroom and began straightening up. It didn't take long. Justin was invariably neat. Only the clothes they'd worn earlier were scattered about. Her negligee and raincoat seemed ludicrous now, when she'd been reduced to wearing one of his shirts. Why hadn't she at least tucked an overnight bag with a change of clothes into the back of the car? Had she planned on leaving here in broad daylight wearing virtually nothing? The truth was, she hadn't thought about leaving at all, only about getting here and stunning him speechless.

She picked up his slacks and when she did, something dropped out of the pocket, then rolled under the bed. She scrambled after it. When her hand closed around it, she realized it was a small velvet box. Her heart stood still.

She rocked back on her heels and stared at the red velvet in wonder. This was what he'd had in mind for tonight, she realized. A romantic dinner and then this. With fingers that trembled, she flipped open the lid and gazed at a stunning solitaire diamond on a wide gold band. Even though the stone was large, there was nothing ostentatious about it. It was elegant and simple, a declaration not just of love, but of understanding.

"He knew," she murmured as tears began to build. He had understood that all of Will's gestures had been for show—the gaudiest diamond, fanciest car, biggest house. This ring just said that Justin Adams loved her and nothing more.

"Oh, Justin," she whispered, her throat tight.

What if she never got to say yes? What if the divorce dragged on, for some reason? What if…? She couldn't bear to say it, not even to think it. Instead, she slid the ring onto her finger. Somehow, she thought, somehow he would know her answer, no matter what. When the decree was final—when Justin was safe— they would start to plan their future.

It was nearly daybreak when she heard the front door open, then close quietly. In a heartbeat, she was on her feet and racing toward the living room. She skidded to a stop at the sight of him. He looked as if he'd been mauled by a particularly cantankerous bull. There were cuts and gashes and dirt. His uniform was in tatters, but he was alive, she told herself. He was blessedly alive.

He glanced up and saw her then and the exhaustion vanished. His eyes lit up.

Patsy moved toward him, then hesitated, all too aware of the state he was in. "How badly are you hurt?"

"Just a few bumps and bruises. The guy took exception to being arrested. I had to chase him down and wrestle around with him near a barbed wire fence. The fence won."

"And you? Did you get your man?"

"Of course," he said, his expression smug. "The good guys always win." He reached for her gingerly, then searched her face. "Don't they?"

"Depends on what they're after, I suppose."

"You know what I'm after," he said. "Are you ready for me to spell it out?"

She held out her hand. "Does it have anything to do with this?"

He stared at the ring in surprise. "You found it?"

"I was straightening up. It fell out of your pocket."

He grinned. "And you assumed it was meant for you?"

She scowled. "And who else would it have been meant for?"

"Maybe some woman who knows her own mind."

"I know my own mind."

"Do you?"

"Always have." She circled his waist with her arms and held on, relishing the sense of security that swept over her. "It just took me a while to figure out I could trust my own judgment. I have had reason to question it, you know."

"You can trust yourself this time, darlin'. I will love you till my dying breath, Patsy Longhorn. I will never hurt you. I will treat Billy as if he were my own and I will make absolutely sure that we have a house crawling with brothers and sisters for him, if that's what you want."

"Oh, it is definitely what I want," she assured him. She gazed into his eyes. "No doubt about it."

He lifted her hand and admired the ring that fit perfectly. "You stole my thunder. I was going to ask you last night," he said. "But you had other plans for the evening."

"I didn't hear any complaints at the time."

"No way. Now, though, I want your full attention. No funny business, okay?"

"Okay."

He surveyed her from the open collar of his shirt

to her bare thighs. She could feel the heat of his gaze everywhere it touched.

"Maybe you ought to get dressed."

She grinned. "My choices are pretty limited. It's this shirt, the negligee or the raincoat."

He groaned. "Never mind. I'll just have to concentrate a little harder."

"Can't remember what you had in mind?" She waved the ring under his nose, then dropped it into his palm. "Does it have anything to do with this?"

Justin looked as if he'd never seen the diamond engagement ring before in his life. "This? Yeah."

His reaction, his inability to focus on anything but her couldn't have pleased her more. Will had always acted as if half his attention was on a speech he had to make later in the day.

"How about the future?" she coached. "Does it have anything to do with that?"

"You're beautiful, you know that."

"The future, together, you and me," she persisted, refusing to allow him to distract her, too.

"Mmm-hmm," he said, and reached for her.

Sometime later, Justin finally managed to get out the words and get the ring on her finger, but the moment was almost anticlimactic. She'd given him her answer long before, in his arms, when she'd murmured yes over and over in his ear. And one day soon, when her divorce was final, the whole world would know, too.

* * *

The wedding plans had been taken completely out of her hands the very instant the divorce decree was final, but for once Patsy wasn't feeling the least bit defensive about losing control over her life. It gave her more time to spend with Justin and Billy, more time to indulge in the incredible romantic fantasy her life had become.

Watching her son with his prospective stepdaddy always brought a lump to her throat. And listening to Will explain to Billy that he would always be his daddy, but that it was okay with him if Billy loved Justin did bring tears to her eyes.

"Thank you," she told Will as he walked to his car after his visit.

"You deserve to be happy. Your being happy will insure that Billy's happy, too. How could I want anything less for my son?" He gazed into her eyes. "There's something I need to thank you for, too."

"What's that?"

"For snapping me back to reality and for agreeing to let Billy spend time with me and my family while you're on your honeymoon. I think it's time both of us learned something about our roots."

"You've always known who you were, Will. You just got lost for a little while."

He grinned sheepishly. "Well, that's one way of looking at it, I suppose." He gave her a peck on the cheek. "Good luck, sweetheart. I think you're getting a better deal this time around."

Patsy didn't say it, but she knew she was. Her gaze

lifted just in time to see Justin coming toward them. Will turned slowly and met Justin's gaze steadily.

"Make her happy," he said.

"I intend to."

"Okay, then, I'll see you two tomorrow night, right after the wedding reception."

"Are you sure you don't want to come?" Patsy said.

"You'd be welcome," Justin added.

Will seemed startled by the sincerity of the gesture. "No, but thanks. Patsy ought to start her new life without a reminder from her old one staring her in the face."

He got into his car then and drove away, leaving Patsy staring after him, her expression thoughtful. "Maybe he's not such a bad person, after all. Maybe it was just the circumstances and the timing."

"I don't know about that," Justin said. "The only timing I'm concerned about now is seeing to it you make it to the church on time tomorrow."

"Sharon Lynn is staying with me. Janet has a time-table posted on the refrigerator door. There's no way I'll be late," she promised.

Of course, she hadn't counted on getting stopped for speeding halfway to the chapel. Even as she hit the brakes, she glanced at the speedometer and noted that she was barely exceeding the posted speed limit.

Ready for an argument, she glanced up into Tate's amused eyes.

"Going somewhere in a hurry, aren't you?"

"You do realize if you keep me out here on the side of the road, I will be late and Justin will worry and the whole family will get in on the act?"

He grinned. "Which is why I decided to be your escort. I don't want any other law enforcement officer coming along and delaying this wedding."

She regarded him curiously. "Why is my marrying Justin so important to you?"

"Because the second you get back from your honeymoon, I'm going to follow Doc Dolan down to the Gulf Coast and spend the rest of my days fishing. Already have my place picked out and my wife's chomping at the bit to get going."

"Which means what for Justin?"

"That he'll be sheriff, if he wants the job."

"Have you told him that?"

"Nope. It's my wedding present. I'll tell him at the reception."

Patsy grinned. "It's better than another blender, I'll give you that."

"Come on, then, girl. We're wasting time. If you're late, Harlan Adams will have the state troopers, the Texas Rangers and Lord knows who else out here looking for you."

When they reached the church, Justin was indeed pacing around outside, with his grandfather right on his heels. The pair of them glared at Tate, who wisely scooted inside without getting dragged into a discussion over his role in her delayed arrival.

''You can go on in now, Grandpa. The wedding's about to start,'' Justin said, his relief evident.

When they were alone, he scowled at her. ''I ought to have you arrested, you know.''

''For what? I haven't done anything.''

''Sure you have. You stole my heart.''

Patsy reached up and cupped his face in her hands. ''For a lawman, you sure do have a way with words.''

And then she kissed him, which is why, forever after, everyone in Los Piños would talk about the fact that Justin Adams kissed his bride before the wedding and almost never made it to the chapel at all.

* * * * *

Watch for Sharon Lynn's emotional story, the next book in the series

AND BABY MAKES THREE: THE NEXT GENERATION:

THE UNCLAIMED BABY,

coming in February as a Silhouette single title release.

Silhouette ® SPECIAL EDITION ®

Newfound sisters Bliss, Tiffany and Katie
learn more about family and true love
than they *ever* expected.

A new miniseries by
LISA JACKSON

A FAMILY KIND OF GUY (SE#1191) August 1998
Bliss Cawthorne wanted nothing to do with ex-flame
Mason Lafferty, the cowboy who had destroyed her
dreams of being his bride. Could Bliss withstand his irre-
sistible charm—the second time around?

A FAMILY KIND OF GAL (SE#1207) November 1998
How could widowed single mother Tiffany Santini be
attracted to her sexy brother-in-law, J.D.? Especially
since J.D. was hiding something that could destroy the
love she had just found in his arms....

And watch for the conclusion of this series in
early 1999 with Katie Kinkaid's story in
A FAMILY KIND OF WEDDING.

Available at your favorite retail outlet. Only from

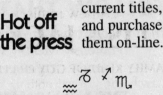

FOLLOW THAT BABY...

the fabulous cross-line series featuring the infamously wealthy Wentworth family...continues with:

THE MILLIONAIRE AND THE PREGNANT PAUPER

by Christie Ridgway
(Yours Truly, 1/99)

When a very expectant mom-to-be from Sabrina Jensen's Lamaze class visits the Wentworth estate with information about the missing heir, her baby is delivered by the youngest millionaire Wentworth, who proposes a marriage of convenience....

Available at your favorite retail outlet, only from

Silhouette®

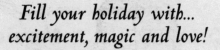

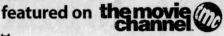

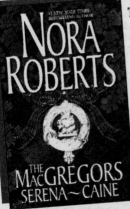
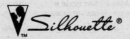

COMING NEXT MONTH

#1219 A FAMILY KIND OF WEDDING—Lisa Jackson
That Special Woman!/Forever Family
When rancher Luke Gates arrived in town on a mysterious mission, he had everything under control—until he lost his heart to hardworking ace reporter Katie Kincaid and her ten-year-old son. Would Katie still trust in him once she learned a shocking secret that would forever alter her family?

#1220 THE MILLIONAIRE BACHELOR—Susan Mallery
During their late-night phone chats, Cathy Eldridge couldn't resist entertaining a pained Stone Ward with tall tales about "her" life as a globe-trotting goddess. Then a twist of fate brought the self-conscious answering-service operator face-to-face with the reclusive millionaire of her dreams....

#1221 MEANT FOR EACH OTHER—Ginna Gray
The Blaines and the McCalls of Crockett, Texas
Good-natured Dr. Mike McCall was only too happy to save Dr. Leah Albright's ailing kid brother. And, as an added bonus, the alluring, ultrareserved lady doc finally allowed Mike to sweep her off her feet. But would their once-in-a-lifetime love survive the ultimate betrayal?

#1222 I TAKE THIS MAN—AGAIN!—Carole Halston
Six years ago, Mac McDaniel had foolishly let the love of his life go. Now he vowed to do anything—and *everything*—to make irresistibly sweet Ginger Honeycutt his again. For better, for worse, he knew they were destined to become husband and wife—for keeps!

#1223 JUST WHAT THE DOCTOR ORDERED—Leigh Greenwood
A hard-knock life had taught Dr. Matt Dennis to steer clear of emotional intimacy at all costs. But when he took a job at a rural clinic, struggling single mom Liz Rawlins welcomed him into her warm, embracing family. Would Liz's tender lovin' care convince the jaded doctor he *truly* belonged?

#1224 PRENUPTIAL AGREEMENT—Doris Rangel
It was meant to be when China Smith blissfully wed the only man she would *ever* love. Though Yance had proposed marriage for the sake of his son, an enamored China planned to cherish her husband forever and always. And she wasn't about to let a pesky prenuptial agreement stand in her way!